VILLAGE LIFE
IS
MURDER

Penelope Chamberlain

First edition printed in the United Kingdom 2023.

A CIP catalogue record of this book is available from the British Library.

ISBN (Hardcover): 9798851849725
ISBN (Paperback): 9798851849565
Imprint: Independently published
Editor: Christine Beech
Typesetting: Matthew J Bird

For further information about this book, please contact the author at:
Pen8chim@aol.com

For Chim and Katrina

ONE

Tuesday night, Wednesday morning

"Bloody village life. I'm going to murder those joyriders!" Seraphina protested.

A high-pitched scream had rudely interrupted her bedtime reading. It was immediately followed by the sound of wheels spinning and a car driving away at speed.

"You said moving here would be peaceful. Pleasant even! No more burglar alarms going off left, right, and centre. No more sirens from passing police and ambulances. And I definitely didn't expect to hear cars race up and down outside my house. It's not even the weekend. But no, it's just the same, isn't it? And you said I'd love living in the countryside!"

Howard chose not to react to the sneering tone in her voice. Maybe she needed more time to adjust to their new situation.

Seraphina shut her book with a sharp snap. "I'm going to sleep now," she announced. "Don't stay up too late; you know the light from your laptop bugs me."

In one swift manoeuvre, she grabbed the lion's share of the quilt, turned her back on her husband, and snuggled down into their antique four-poster bed.

"Goodnight," said Howard quietly. As he tapped away, he recorded the events of the day.

Another peaceful, uneventful day. Just how I like it. It's just a shame Seraphina hasn't settled yet, but I'm sure she will.

After musing over the day, Howard decided there was no more to add. He clicked 'Save', closed his laptop, and quietly turned off the bedside lamp before settling down to sleep.

Morning arrived, and Howard was in the kitchen loading the dishwasher when Seraphina rushed down the stairs, exclaiming, "Why didn't you tell me it was time I was gone?" She grabbed her coat off the back of the kitchen chair, where she'd left it the day before, and shouted through the house as she went, "I've got to dash now. See you tonight."

Howard called back from the kitchen, "OK, have a nice day. Don't let the front door slam."

It did, with a loud bang. Seraphina immediately called through the letterbox apologetically, "Sorry. See you later," before she set off on her 10-minute walk to work.

Scanning the room to make sure the kitchen was tidy, Howard grabbed his favourite long navy jacket from the cupboard in the hallway. He slipped it on and headed for the door. Every day after Seraphina went to work, he visited the local newspaper-cum-coffee shop. Today was no exception.

"Good morning," greeted June, the shopkeeper. "How are you today?" Without waiting for an answer, she delighted in telling him how busy she'd been that morning. "Without Barbara's help, I'm rushed off my feet. Do you know how long it takes to sort these newspapers every morning?"

Howard went to answer but, again, she didn't wait for a reply and continued, "An hour every morning! It all goes on behind the scenes, you know. My lovely customers, just like you Howard, come in here every day to collect your paper and you see me, like a swan. I'm all calm on top, yet I'm paddling away like mad underneath to keep this busy metropolis of daily activity afloat." She smiled at him and held her look just a little longer than necessary. Howard chuckled to himself at her description of the archetypical village corner shop.

"Well, I think you do a grand job, June. Can l have my usual latte when you've got a minute, please? And I'll take this paper, thanks."

He went to his favourite window seat and spread the newspaper on the table, intending to take in the daily headlines. Today was different, though. Instead of flicking through the pages like he normally did, he just gazed out of the window onto the village green. He enjoyed watching everyone go about their business and smiled to himself without even realising it. He watched the kids as they boarded the school bus and the usual collection of commuters making their way to the train station. A very familiar routine that, fortunately, was now part of his past.

Now and then, he casually glanced over in June's direction to check on the progress of his latte. Service was slow today, but he didn't mind. He wasn't in a rush to be anywhere special. Eventually, she arrived with his coffee and found him still smiling.

"And what's so good that it's put a smile on your face this morning, then?"

"Ah, June, just watching you swan around!"

"Cheeky one today, aren't you?" She gently placed his coffee on the table in front of him and leaned in a little closer saying, "I need to keep a close eye on you today, don't I?" She winked at him and smiled, as she trotted back to the counter, asking loudly as she went, "Who's next please?"

June was in her early 60s. She dyed her grey hair a strawberry-blond shade of red, which she kept long but piled high on top of her head. She was not very tall, but carried herself with a confidence that exaggerated her height, as did her hair.

Howard wondered why such a remarkably stylish lady ran a corner shop in a backwater countryside village. Kind, with a friendly face, she always wore full-face makeup. He had once overheard a customer compliment her appearance to which she had replied, with her best thespian voice, "You just never know whom you might bump into, so one must always look one's best, Darling, regardless of the hour!"

June always looked for a happy-ever-after in stories of woe. People confided in her and, on occasions, she became an unofficial local Relate councillor, or so Barbara had told Howard on one of her infrequent front-of-shop appearances.

Howard had only lived in the village a few months, with his wife of 21 years, but he had already seen June handing out her version of, 'If I were you, what I would do…' therapy to several customers. She was like the village mum; a natural chatterbox but pleasant with a heart of gold. She had quickly grown fond of Howard and had taken him under her wing.

Another morsel of information, passed on by Barbara, was that June was known to be a flirt and a bit of a cougar. Barbara was June's shop assistant and rarely greeted customers, only when refilling the shelves. Howard had often wondered why. Maybe she was shy. Or maybe June preferred to keep her out the back because of her gossipy nature. Either way, he couldn't help but speculate about the dynamics between them. He enjoyed his latte as he happily watched customers come and go.

Suddenly, there was a loud bang on the shop door. As he looked up, he saw a woman on crutches almost smash the glass in the door, as her shoulder bag swung around in front of her. She was out of breath as she spluttered out her words, "Whoops, sorry about that! Any chance of a coffee to go, June? I've got to catch the next train to the city, and, at my speed, it'll be touch and go if I make it."

Howard vaguely recognised her. During his walks with his dog, Charlie, he had exchanged the occasional "Good morning" with her. Although, strangely, until today, he had never noticed how pretty she was and could not remember seeing her in the shop before. He astounded himself as he swiftly finished his coffee, folded his paper under his arm, and jumped up quickly, saying,

"Hi, I've seen you before, haven't I? Can I be of any help? I'm not doing much this morning, so I could help you to the station if you like."

He paused as a slight nervousness washed over him and he realised what he'd just proposed. He quickly decided that he should make good his offer.

"I used to be a commuter so I appreciate how those trains don't wait for anyone, do they? Here, let me carry your bags for you, so you don't have to struggle to the station."

They looked at each other and seemed equally surprised at the impromptu offer. Eventually, after what seemed like an age to him, June broke the silence. "Your coffee, Sarah, and it seems it comes with a free 'knight in shining armour' this morning." She winked at Sarah and, in a reassuring tone, said, "You'll be quite safe with Howard, I'm sure."

Sarah thanked June for being so quick, as she took the coffee and blushed ever so slightly at her comment. As she turned to Howard, she was in half a mind to decline his offer but, with the coffee in her hand, she realised she hadn't thought it through and could do with some help. It was her first day back at work since her accident and she hadn't considered what a struggle it might be.

Meanwhile, Howard's confidence had returned. With a cheerful, but calm tone, he said, "Pass me your coffee and let me get the door for starters." He felt particularly pleased with himself now that he had something, or someone, to make his morning a little more interesting.

Sarah handed him the coffee and adjusted the bag over her shoulder, hoping it would stay in place this time. As she turned towards the door, Howard was already there, holding it open. She tried to be graceful but hobbled through the doorway awkwardly on her crutches. Howard nodded in June's direction and called out, "I'll see you tomorrow, June. Have a great day."

June looked up. She wanted to appear busy, restocking the counter with sweets, whilst Howard took control of the 'Sarah situation'. She remained silent but smiled a knowing smile and raised her eyebrows slightly. As she gave a small wave, she made a mental note to find out the following day how it all went.

"Let me introduce myself properly. My name is Howard and I live in the village. Actually, I've only lived here for a few months. Did I hear June say that your name is Sarah?"

He tried to be as cheerful and confident as he could muster. It wasn't like him to be nervous, as he had always been a confident go-getter.

"Yes," said Sarah. "I've seen you when I've walked my dog, haven't I? It's very kind of you to help me. I think I was on autopilot when I called in for a coffee. The things we do out of habit. I'm an idiot! It never crossed my mind how I was going to carry it to the station. But don't you have somewhere to be?"

Howard muttered, "No, not really."

Realising how feeble he sounded, he quickly continued, "Well, not this morning, anyway. Dare I ask how you ended up with your foot in plaster, struggling on crutches?"

Sarah paused. There was no way she was going to tell him what had happened.

"I'm so clumsy," she said. "I'd put a magazine on the stairs and meant to take it up with me next time I went. I forgot it was there and slipped on it. I came down so awkwardly that I broke my ankle. I only slipped down a couple of steps as well!"

She impressed herself with how she had perfected her story since her initial visit to A&E and how convincing she sounded.

It was only a short walk to the train station. As Howard walked, and Sarah hobbled along on her crutches, they chatted pleasantly about broken bones and how quickly they mend.

"That's me, platform 2, over there. How typical, I'll have to take the lift. I'm not very good at steps with these crutches. Ironic really, as it was the stairs that got me into this mess. Here comes the lift now. I'll hop in. I'll be fine from here, thanks."

Howard wasn't happy to leave her at the lift and insisted, "No, I'll come with you to your carriage and make sure you're properly settled, if that's okay?"

He wanted to make sure she was safely on board before he left her, and almost ended up with an impromptu day trip to the city, but he managed to jump off just in time.

As the train pulled away, Sarah waved from the window. She looked at Howard and thought he reminded her of someone but couldn't figure out who.

Howard waved back and momentarily indulged his imagination that the pretty Sarah was his girlfriend and he walked her to the station every day.

Foregoing the lift on his return, he crossed the platform via the steps and bridge. As he did so, he noticed the detailed architecture of the Victorian station. Even the handrails had swirling leaves in cast iron, each painted green and interspersed with red roses. How elaborate for a small village train station, he thought, and wondered why he had never noticed it before, but he liked it. Howard liked everything about the village, and today he liked it just a little more.

Pleased with himself to have helped a stranger, he walked tall with an all-round-feel-good smile on his face.

As he strolled across the bridge, he had felt a strange sensation of disconnection from his earlier life until he caught sight of a man rushing. He was wearing a long navy jacket and carrying a black rucksack over his shoulder, just like Howard used to. He was immediately reminded of his old life and his commuting days. He briefly wondered whether the commuter intended to catch the same train as Sarah but, if so, he had already missed it.

Thoughts of his old life soon faded as he left the station, and the warm rays of the morning sun warmed him during his leisurely walk home.

TWO

Wednesday morning

Seraphina desperately missed her old life and yearned for the familiar buzz of excitement that hummed through the city streets. When she had worked in London, she had felt part of something bigger and loved to be surrounded by intelligent, career-minded people. She was twenty-five when she first met Howard, who was two years her senior. Already a successfully established trader on the floor, he had impressed her with his energy and style. She could see by his designer clothes that he was doing well and success was an extremely attractive quality to her. She was smitten with his lifestyle and company. After a whirlwind romance, they were married within a year.

Much to Howard's disappointment they were never blessed with children, or their associated expense. Nice cars, luxury holidays, and life's treats had become the norm for Seraphina for the last twenty years. That was the life she had signed up for. Not for it all to end abruptly when Howard reached burnout point, and his doctor recommended that he walk away and find a less stressful life.

Finally, after many lengthy discussions, they reached a mutual decision. They resolved to pack up and move to the countryside, where they would take some time out before looking for new jobs. Perhaps interesting part-time roles to keep their brains active. Seraphina even joked about contacting one of the TV shows that help people find a new home in the country.

After accepting their 'joint' decision, she attempted to embrace the situation. She even looked forward to becoming a lady of leisure for a while. She gathered information about the local sports centre and collected leaflets about various classes and activities. It particularly excited her to discover an exclusive spa resort nearby.

In short, she found her last few weeks in the office positively liberating. She had loved telling her colleagues about the life of leisure she was about to have, and everyone appeared to be envious.

By the time they came to move, she was looking forward to it, rather than her initial apprehension when she was concerned about what she would leave behind. She had visions of enjoying the opportunity to unwind, explore her new surroundings, and meet new people.

How wrong she was.

One Sunday afternoon, in the first two weeks of arriving in the village, they decided to check out the local pub and Seraphina walked away with a job offer.

Debbie, the landlady, was never one to miss an opportunity. She knew that Chris's current accountant was due to retire, so was quick to introduce him to Seraphina. They hit it off straight away and, by the time they finished their drinks, she had been interviewed and agreed to pop into his office the following day to iron out the finer details.

Debbie had explained to them that local jobs, other than farming, were exceptionally rare, so an accountancy opportunity was not to be missed. When Chris offered her the job, Howard was thrilled, saying, "What timing. What luck. It was meant to be."

While he harped on about how the location was perfect, only a 10-minute walk from their house, and what a nice guy Chris seemed to be, Seraphina was silently battling with her emotions. It was all she could do to stop herself from telling him to accept the job offer himself, as he was evidently so excited about it.

However, after a slow walk home, she had to admit that the timing of the role was uncanny, and Chris seemed like a genuinely nice guy. They were sure the post wouldn't come up again soon and decided that, as long as she could negotiate a suitable package, she would accept the job.

She bargained hard and arranged the start date to be in a couple of weeks. While it gave her a little more time off, it was a fraction compared to what she had imagined. Sadly, she had to admit that she would be crazy to turn the job down as it ticked a lot of boxes.

Meanwhile, Howard managed the renovation work on their new house. Once completed, he was able to enjoy the freedom she had imagined for herself. Now, several months later, and much to her disappointment, he still hadn't started looking for a job.

After her mad dash out of the house that morning, she made it to work on time. The office was just off the village high street, so there was not much passing traffic or trade. Chris was out meeting a potential new client, which meant she had the office to herself for a while, and could get her head down and concentrate. Balancing some clients' accounts was a work of art, and she appreciated being able to focus without distraction.

The silence was not to last though. By mid-morning, her idyllic solitude was shattered by the jangling of the traditional shop bell on the front door. Chris had kept the bell when he took the building on as it added a certain vintage charm, plus it was handy to know if anyone came in when he was in the upstairs office.

With the silence broken, Seraphina looked up to see a very tall, exceptionally tatty, yet substantially muscular figure of a man as he bounded into the office. He wore the most bizarre combination of clothes she had ever seen. It would have been easy to mistake him for a homeless person. He reminded her of the people that used to ask for money as she crossed Blackfriars Bridge on her way to her old job. He wore brown trousers which once must have belonged to a half-decent suit but were now only fit for the ragman. Not even a charity shop would have accepted them. His shirt was dog-eared at the collar points. His jacket was so stretched out of shape it was almost impossible to tell if it belonged to the trousers. He completed his look with a pair of tired, well-worn Hunter wellington boots, covered in what she hoped was just mud. She stood up and offered a handshake to introduce herself.

"Ah ha," bellowed the man. "You'll be Chris's new lady then. Seraphina. Am I right?" She managed a quick nod and was about to reply when the man talked over her. "Ah, you're just as beautiful as Chris described you."

Instead of shaking her outstretched hand, he thrust a tatty dog-eared shoe box into it. "There you go. I think you'll find everything is in order. I expect you can fire your way through that lot in a day. A woman of your calibre, it won't take you long, will it?"

The box had seen better days and it was so full that the lid wouldn't close, with paper sticking out from all four sides.

She was as unimpressed with his familiar approach as she was with his appearance. As she looked at the papers poking out of the box, she deduced that this very tall, loud man had to be Mr Palmer. Chris had mentioned that he might visit today but, based on his affectionate description, she hadn't expected the dishevelled appearance of the man who boldly strode into the office.

She stared at the shoe box which Mr Palmer had energetically and confidently thrust at her and tried to think of something polite to say.

With enthusiasm, he said, "I say, Miss Seraphina. You'll be alright with this, won't you?"

She looked up, frustrated and annoyed on so many levels. He had disturbed her peace, the presentation of his accounts was disappointing and what did he think he was doing calling her 'Miss'?

She felt patronised and couldn't stop herself. She took a deep breath and tried to sound as professional and as confident as she could. "How nice to meet you, Mr Palmer. Yes, my name is Seraphina Buchanan. Now, if you presented your accounts in a more orderly fashion than an old shoe box, I would be able to complete the task faster for you."

She frowned, not very enthralled with the job ahead of her. She had never experienced it, but she had heard stories of how some folk were disorganised with their accounts because they were behind with technology. Her old job in the city was paperless, having embraced all things digital several years ago, and today she missed it.

Just then, the little bell jangled over the front door and Chris walked in, back from his appointment. He looked incredibly pleased with himself and was delighted to find his friend in the office. "Hello, Ziggy. How are you? All good, I hope."

Out of the corner of his eye, he saw the infamous box on Seraphina's desk. "Ah, the trusty old shoe box again, is it? How many years have you used that now?" He laughed as he turned to Seraphina.

"I see you've met Ziggy then. I'm sure you two will get along famously."

"Ziggy, this is Seraphina, the new accountant I told you about. She comes to us with a wealth of experience from the city. She's got a great eye for detail, so if you've tried any of your usual creative accounting or you've thrown in any of those random expenses, you've got her to deal with this time!"

Chris smiled, and Ziggy gave a loud belly laugh. "Would I do that?" he replied, as he flashed Seraphina an enormous, friendly smile. As he turned and headed for the door, he held his hand high, gesturing a backward wave. "Goodbye, my darlings," he announced loudly, as he tapped the bell above the door and laughed to himself as he left.

Seraphina turned to Chris, as she sat back in her chair and crossed her arms in front of her. With a smidgen of disapproval in her voice, she sighed. "Well, he wasn't at all what I expected. You know, he never introduced himself; I had to guess who he was. And his appearance was most unusual as well." She tilted her head to one side, raised her left eyebrow and, with her arms still folded, she continued. "You never mentioned he was called Ziggy, either. So, how did he get his name?"

"Well, where do I start? With a drink, I think. Do you want one?"

She didn't reply as he sauntered over to the small kitchen area which was set behind a low wall at the rear of the office. He picked up his mug and placed it on the drinks machine tray. He carefully ran his finger up and down the vast selection of drink pods before he selected a mocha coffee and inserted the pod into the machine.

Apart from his height, Chris bore no resemblance to Ziggy. He was a contemporary individual who always wore the latest eye-catching style. With her keen eye for designer clothes, she could tell when they had first met that he was a successful business owner, casual yet confident. He wore his salt-and-pepper hair neatly jelled back and had a goatee beard and moustache. The silver tones in his hair set off his pale blue eyes. She thought he oozed class and sophistication; a look she felt was only achieved with a good upbringing and solid education. A look she admired and appreciated. The same look that had attracted her to Howard all those years ago when they first met in the office.

Chris was not perturbed by her obvious disappointment with their visitor. "Ziggy and I go back a long way, to primary school. We've always called him Ziggy, but no one remembers where the nickname came from. You're not the first to ask. It's kind of in keeping with his personality and I think it suits him. What do you think?"

Since Ziggy was a good friend to Chris, Seraphina decided it would be wise to set aside her first impression and initial annoyance. "Well, I wouldn't like to comment. I've only just met him." She was proud to be professional but maybe, on this occasion, her slight outburst hadn't been. "I'll let you know my thoughts when I've sorted his shoe box. As you know, you can learn a lot from someone's accounts," she said, smiling.

"Well, you could've fooled me. It sounded like you'd already made your mind up. You'll speak to him again soon though, and I know you'll like him once you get to know him. Everyone does." Chris grinned as he held up her office mug and gave it a little wiggle. "You want a coffee or not, then?"

He was such a kind person that she couldn't stay angry at him for long. "Go on then, make mine a latte, please. It'll keep me going until lunch. I'm starving today."

After Ziggy's loud visit, they settled down to work until Chris received a call from another prospective client. Keen to never miss an opportunity to sign up a new account, he dashed out to a meeting and peace returned to the office.

While Seraphina got on with her work uninterrupted, Ziggy's appearance replayed in her mind several times that afternoon. He may have looked like a tramp, but there was something about him. He was tall and muscular and, although his dark wavy hair was unkempt, he had a rugged handsomeness about him which she wasn't used to.

THREE

Mid Wednesday morning

After Howard waved the beautiful Sarah off at the train station, he returned home to collect Charlie and take him for his daily walk. As he crossed the green and headed for the path alongside the river, he thought about dinner options for that evening. He was now in the habit of having a cooked dinner ready for when Seraphina arrived home from work.

This morning though, he found it hard to focus as his thoughts soon drifted away from recipes and back to Sarah. The unexpected trip to the train station earlier, and the sharp reminder of his old life, made him recall the reason for all the upheaval. As he meandered through the last six months, he thought about how far he and Seraphina had come in such a short time and wondered if it had all been for the better.

He had project-managed the restoration of their new home and got to know the area and a few of the local characters. To search for a job was not a current priority for him, much to Seraphina's disgust.

What started as a small spark of envy had grown over the last few months. He even described her as *the green-eyed monster* in his diary just a few days ago. Luckily, she never read his diary. She always said it was pointless and had vowed never to be tempted to read it, even behind his back. Regardless, he kept his password secret; especially as she seemed to be losing her patience with him a lot lately.

Now that the renovations were completed, he took care of the housework. He also prepared the dinner, ready for her return at the end of each day. What more did she want? If he was honest with himself, he knew. It didn't matter how much money they had in the bank; she wanted him to get a job because she had one.

Sadly, his conversation was becoming limited. To avoid confrontation, Seraphina's solution was to go to bed before him. She would make sure she was asleep and, if not, would have her nose buried in a book when he came up.

He was not happy with the way things had turned out. He knew they were drifting apart, but he had another goal to achieve before he found a job. He concluded that maybe they would get used to their new life together with time.

As he walked back with Charlie, he decided to cook her favourite meal that evening. She loved lamb chops with creamy mash and sugar snap peas, all washed down with a perfectly chilled, crisp glass of rosé wine. Without thinking, he picked up his pace and blazed straight across the cricket field into the village butchers, with Charlie in tow.

His quick decision ruffled Spencer's feathers. The cricket team captain had just arrived to check the conditions for the mid-week game. He shouted over to Howard as he stomped over his hallowed green. Howard, however, was so focused that he did not hear him.

His arrival at the butcher's shop caused more upset. "Park that dog outside," shouted the butcher. "I love dogs, but I can't have them in the shop nowadays. Quick, quick, before the wife sees."

Robbo slammed his exceedingly sharp cleaver straight through a large joint of beef, cutting it clean in half in one swift slice. Howard didn't want to get on the wrong side of Robbo or his cleaver. He was quick to apologise and hastily tied Charlie up outside.

"Health and safety, mate," said Robbo, as Howard returned to the counter. "Right, let's try that again, shall we? Good morning, Howard." As he looked up at the oversized clock on the shop wall, he continued, "Actually, it's more like lunchtime now, isn't it? Can I tempt you to some sausages or maybe some back bacon for brunch?"

"Not today, Robbo. I'm after some lamb chops. The best you have, please."

"You're pushing the boat out for a mid-week meal, aren't you? What's the special occasion? Not that there needs to be one. Lamb just isn't the cheapest option nowadays, is it? Not that I'm complaining. I love a customer with good taste. You know, I remember when lamb …" Robbo continued to talk about how the price of lamb had fallen and risen over the years whilst he carefully selected four generously sized chops.

Meanwhile, Howard's attention was caught by a man walking past the shop window, with a dog like Sarah's. He was sure it was hers, especially as Charlie appeared to know it. He was curious, was the man Sarah's husband or a dog walker? Howard hadn't noticed if she was married. There had been no mention of a significant other when they spoke, but then, why should she? Although, if she had a partner, why was she hobbling unassisted?

Just then, Robbo interrupted his thoughts and drew him sharply back into the present. "… a bit like your stock exchange, Howard. But you'd know all about that, wouldn't you?"

"Sorry? What was that about the exchange?"

"The price of lamb, Mate. Going up and down, just like your old stock exchange."

"Yes, an interesting parallel," said Howard, as he agreed and smiled politely.

Robbo held the chops out for approval before he gently placed them on the scales and announced, "That's £8.52." He said it as more of a statement than a question and assumed Howard's approval. He wrapped the lamb chops in greaseproof paper before he sealed the neatly presented parcel with a bespoke sticky label. Howard appreciated the presentation and compared it to when he used to shop at Fortnum & Mason, although this was on a considerably smaller scale.

"You know, I do regularly have lamb cutlets, which you might like to try sometime. Is that all?"

"Yes, thanks, that's all for today."

Robbo held out the card machine for payment. Being a naturally nosey fellow, he tried to pry once more, as he asked, "What's the special occasion then?"

"Oh, no reason. I just thought we'd have a pleasant night at home together."

"Ah, I see. I reckon you're on a promise there then, Mate. Let me know if the lamb does the trick!" he replied, while laughing loudly at his own suggestive comment.

As friendly as he was, Robbo was prone to exaggerate and easily made the ordinary sound extraordinary. Howard did not want to volunteer any additional information to fuel his overactive imagination. Although it was entertaining to listen to his elaborate tales, he didn't want to be the inspiration for one.

Butchery techniques were where Robbo's skills lay, and he was the king of his castle when he was behind his counter. He was proud to be the village butcher and often contributed to local events.

Despite being surrounded by a fine array of produce, he maintained a steady weight and stood tall at about 5 feet 10 inches. His hair was mousey-brown, with a few scattered grey hairs around his temples. He was a friendly guy, and Howard enjoyed supporting his business. The crown of lamb he had bought a few months ago had been impressive. That was when he had wanted to surprise Seraphina with a lovely meal to celebrate the kitchen's completion. Robbo had done an excellent job and Howard had not forgotten.

He thanked him for the chops and, after he untied Charlie, he made his way to the greengrocers. Howard was a sociable guy and found the village a very friendly place, unlike the city, where no one would say 'Good morning', let alone stop and have a chat. A quick trip to the shops could frequently last an entire afternoon. Seraphina had once commented it was like they had stepped back in time. While Howard enjoyed it, it was clear that it would take some time for her to get used to it.

The greengrocers was only a short walk down the high street from the butchers and, this time, Howard remembered to tie Charlie up outside.

Pauline was busy arranging the carrot display when he arrived. She was super friendly, and he had got on well with her from the first time they met. She was in her early forties with wild, curly, dark blond hair. Not too tall and, at first glance, she looked a little tubby until you realised it was all muscle, built by carting the fruit and vegetables around. Howard had once offered to help when he saw her carry 25kg sacks of potatoes. She declined and told him that it was not a problem for her, as it was part of her daily gym routine and she wanted to burn the calories.

He headed straight for the sugar snap peas and potatoes. He browsed for a short time, before making his way to the counter to pay. Just as he placed his items on the counter, the man he had seen with the dog earlier, rushed in.

"Pauline, have you got any mushrooms?" he asked, as he looked Howard up and down. Quickly peeking out of the window to see if Charlie had company again, Howard was surprised to see him sitting patiently alone.

"If you don't mind, Mike, I think you'll find this gentleman was here before you," Pauline replied, nodding towards Howard. A little stunned at the man's nerve, Howard replied, "Oh, that's okay. Please, go ahead," as he stepped back from the counter and allowed the man to cut in.

Pauline served him as quickly as she could and watched Mike in silence as he rushed out of the door. Once out of earshot, she said, "Sorry about him. I'd like to say it doesn't happen much but, unfortunately, Mike's always in a rush and often appears rude. I think it's because he doesn't like to talk to people, so he does everything quickly! I've known him to spend an entire evening in the local pub and only speak to order his drink. He seems to communicate most of the time with just a nod or a grunt, unless something has got him rattled, then he's very vocal!"

"No problem," said Howard, who secretly wanted to ask if he was Sarah's husband but didn't want to draw attention to his thoughts. Instead, he paid for his goods and thanked Pauline.

"Who's a good boy, then?" he asked, as he rubbed Charlie's head before untying him from the pet hook and making their way home.

The rest of the day passed quickly. He made sure the house was clean and tidy, before spending time in the study on his PC. Before he knew it, it was time to get dinner ready.

Cooking in the newly-enlarged kitchen was a source of joy for him. Originally, the house had been two small semi-detached stone cottages. They had been knocked into one property but had become a large, disorganised rabbit warren. Howard and Seraphina had seen the potential in the space. It was the property that ultimately decided them on this village, along with its convenient train station. Seraphina had insisted they find a place with a direct route into the city, in case either of them wanted to return to work. While Howard initially thought she was considering his career, he now wondered if she had been thinking of herself.

As soon as they moved in, they engaged the services of an architect and decided that Howard would be the project manager. They wanted to invest in the area by using local trades and businesses, as well as getting to know everyone at the same time.

Their kitchen was handmade and fitted by Marty, a well-known local character who was also an excellent, well-respected and frequently recommended cabinet maker. His work impressed them, especially his ability to make cabinets fit the wonky walls in their old cottage.

They ended up with a handmade, hand-painted oak kitchen with bespoke marble work surfaces and a Belfast sink. Seraphina loved it. Most of the kitchen had been her choice, while Howard's role was to oversee the work. He also spent a lot of time rearranging furniture in an attempt to keep the house liveable through it all. He joked once to Seraphina about how she was the lucky one, being able to go to work and escape the mess. Sadly, she hadn't seen the funny side.

It all turned out well in the end, though, and they had the most gorgeous country cottage, which Howard loved. The garden was to be the next challenge.

He checked his watch. Seraphina was late. As he gazed out of the diamond-leaded kitchen window, he could hear the saucepan lid rattle. It would soon be time to mash the potatoes, but he didn't want to overcook the chops. He had done that once before and she said it was like trying to eat an old leather shoe.

All he could do was wait.

******

It was almost closing time when Chris returned to the office, very pleased with himself. He had gained two new clients that day and wanted to celebrate. He insisted they go to the pub for a quick drink. To ensure Seraphina wasn't late home, they closed the office early.

She liked his approach. He was her kind of boss and, for just a moment, it felt like city life again - work hard and play hard. They arrived at the pub suited and booted, but the local clientele wasn't. Football was on the TV, and it had drawn in quite a few local characters. Mr Palmer, alias Ziggy, was one of them, still looking quite the tramp.

"I wasn't expecting you to be here," said Chris, as he passed Ziggy on his way to the bar. "I guess you'd like a pint as well, then? Seraphina, what are you having?"

"I'll have a gin and tonic, please. Thank you."

Ziggy walked over to join them. His voice boomed as he said, "We meet again, my dear, and so soon." He followed with a gracious bow that would have been better suited to an 18th-century court. Rising, he gently kissed the back of her hand. It shocked her that such a scruffy person could behave so graciously. She couldn't work him out.

"Have you delved into my accounts yet, my dear?" he asked, suggestively.

"I need to finish my current case, Mr Palmer. Then I'll get to yours at some point tomorrow."

"Oh, please don't call me 'Mr Palmer'. That's just so formal. Now you're working for Chris, we're practically family." She thought it was a strange comment, but Chris had said that they had known each other since they were children.

Chris soon appeared with the drinks, and they chatted about the new clients and what they needed, mixed with a few choice words of football commentary. After a swift couple of drinks and a few introductions by Chris and Ziggy, Seraphina made her excuses and left them to their pints and football.

She didn't want Howard to be jealous of her brief trip to the pub, so she decided it would be best not to mention it, although dashing quickly home had sent the alcohol straight to her head. As she entered the kitchen, she could see Howard gazing out of the window. It was on the tip of her tongue to make a sarcastic comment until she noticed how beautiful the table looked. As she was slightly late, she thought better of it. "Hello there, this looks nice. What's the special occasion?" she asked, hoping that he was about to announce that he had found a job.

"No special reason, really. I just thought we'd have a lovely night together and start with your favourite meal." He hoped she would be pleased as he popped the chops under the grill and walked to the fridge. As he opened the door to grab the perfectly chilled bottle of Zinfandel, she picked up a glass from the dining table.

"Yes, please. A large one to get me started then," she said, as she was desperate to cover the smell of alcohol on her breath and thought the wine would help.

The meal was perfect, just as Howard had hoped. The alcohol had taken its effect on Seraphina, and she became quite chatty. She told him about Ziggy and explained how she couldn't work him out.

"Chris, my boss," which was her subtle way of pointing out that she had a boss while he still didn't, "described him as coming from a wealthy background, with a public-school education, so I expected him to be smartly presented. I never for one minute thought he'd turn up looking like a tramp!"

She described his clothes, attitude, hair and eyes before Howard interrupted her. "Hold on a minute, just how long did you spend with this guy? I thought you said you didn't like him. Either way, he seems to have made a pretty powerful impression on you!"

"Oh, not long," she protested. "It was the only thing of interest that happened today." She reached for the bottle and refilled her glass. The wine was going down fast.

As she spoke, a seed of curiosity was beginning to grow about Mr Palmer, alias Ziggy. She didn't understand why, and pushed the thought to the back of her mind. She told herself that the country air must have got to her, or was it the two large glasses of wine on top of the earlier gin and tonics, which she had still not mentioned to Howard?

She tried to change the subject, but the best she could do was, "Anyway, what did you get up to today? The weather was wonderful, wasn't it?"

It seemed to work.

"Not a lot. I had my usual trip to the corner shop for the newspaper, walked the dog, and did a bit of shopping. Nothing special, really. But this is making up for it now." He smiled and topped up her glass with the last of the wine.

"Oh no, how did that happen? I didn't realise I drank so much so quickly! I've got a new client coming in first thing tomorrow and I want to go in early and get things ready. I shouldn't have drunk all that on a school night!"

"You were obviously enjoying it, Seraphina. Don't worry about it. I promise I'll bring you a nice cup of tea in bed in the morning to help you get up," he smiled.

Before they knew it, the 10 o'clock news popped up on the TV, which was the trigger for her bedtime.

"I don't know where this evening's gone to. I'm off to bed."

She turned off the lamp on the table next to her, picked up her handbag, plumped up the cushions on her sofa and headed, with a slight stagger, for the stairs. "Don't stay up too late, will you?" she called over her shoulder as she climbed the stairs.

Howard decided he would go up as well, rather than the separate bedtimes they had become used to lately. He turned off the TV, sorted Charlie for the night, locked up the house, and headed up the stairs.

He thought he was quick and not that far behind her, but he must have misjudged his timing as, when he reached the bedroom, it was already in darkness. It disappointed him greatly to find her clothes in a pile on the floor, with her already snuggled in bed. He thought the evening had gone well and had visions of them chatting for a while, like they used to.

Instead, he quietly turned on his bedside lamp and got ready for bed. He didn't want to disturb her, as it looked like she was asleep. He gently slid into bed, reached for his laptop, and updated his diary.

Interesting day. I am disappointed with Seraphina this evening, especially after I'd made such an effort. How could such a lovely evening end so abruptly? Why was she so quick to head up to bed?

He retraced the events of his day, and it wasn't long before his thoughts turned to the beautiful Sarah. Would he see her again tomorrow morning, and would she have anyone there to help her? He wondered why he was thinking about another woman when he was in the marital bed, with his wife lying next to him. He glanced over as she shuffled in her sleep and muttered something as she turned.

Yes, he thought, after all the effort he had gone to that evening, he would help Sarah tomorrow. He decided he would get up early to make sure.

FOUR

Thursday morning

The day began as usual for Seraphina. Even though the alarm woke her at 7 am, Howard was already up and had walked into the bedroom with the cup of tea he had promised.

"Morning. I'm surprised to see you up before the alarm." As she spoke, she felt the words rattle through her skull.

"I thought I might walk you to work as it's a lovely day. Shame to waste it, and I promised you a cup of tea in bed, didn't I?"

"Er, well, yes, you did. Thanks," she replied, wondering if it was going to be such a lovely day with her head banging.

Howard headed downstairs and shouted over his shoulder, "Fancy a bacon and egg sandwich?"

There was no reply. Then his mobile pinged with a text from Seraphina. "Yes, please. Thank you. I'll be down in a minute."

She thought this was a handy alternative to yelling through the house, especially today.

They often texted each other from one room to another. Sound barely travelled through the house as the walls were so thick. They used to walk the length of the house just to find out if the other wanted a cup of tea. When they planned the alterations, they thought it would be a clever idea to have the kitchen at one end of the house and the office at the other. If either was to ever work from home, the last thing they wanted was to be next to the kitchen, as it would be a temptation to just nip in. They used the snug as their home office, where Howard spent an increasing amount of time. So the texting began. Lazy maybe, but convenient, especially this morning.

Seraphina thought a cooked breakfast was a bonus and hoped it would go some way to cure what she now realised was, unquestionably, a hangover. What did she have at the pub that had such an effect on her? As she ate her breakfast, she totted up her drinks from the night before; two gin and tonics, and an entire bottle of wine. No wonder she felt rough.

Meanwhile, she could hear Howard rattling on about what a lovely day it was; something about how he wanted to be out in the fresh air as much as possible; how getting up early with her was a good start to the day and he might do it more often. As her attention returned to the room, she heard him say, "And I get to spend time with my lovely wife."

She began to feel guilty about the previous night's behaviour, but couldn't muster the energy to join in any decent conversation. Her head felt like her brain was loose inside her skull and jangling around like the steel ball in a pinball game when she spoke.

Meanwhile, Howard felt somewhat guilty about his plans for that morning and wondered if he was overcompensating. Was he just paranoid because of his guilt? He decided not to say anymore and finished his cup of tea in silence. If only he had known how remote Seraphina felt this morning, he wouldn't have given his guilty feelings the time of day.

She looked up and mustered a smile. "Come on then, let's get a wiggle on. I want to get in early today, remember?"

Of course he had remembered. That was why he was up first and made a cup of tea, not so that he could make sure he was at the corner shop nice and early.

As they set off together, the fresh air was most welcomed by Seraphina. It made her feel a little more human. Forever the optimist, Howard tried to spark up a conversation again. "Got any déjà vu?"

Seraphina partially nodded, so he tried once more. "Just like old times, isn't it? Walking to work together but without the train ride."

After a momentary pause, she replied, "Yes, but I'm surprised you didn't bring Charlie. You could have gone on a lovely walk with him afterwards."

"I don't think June likes dogs in her shop, and I'm going to get the paper when I leave you. You know I like to support her and have a latte when I call in."

Seraphina looked at him out of the corner of her eye, confused. "Oh, I thought you tied him up outside. I'm sure you've taken him before, haven't you?"

He had plans and had deliberately left Charlie at home. He muttered something about how he would check with June again when he was there. He didn't want to dwell on it as he knew his reply was lame, but it was the first thing that had come to mind.

Arriving at Seraphina's office, Howard said, "Have a great day then." Just as she was about to reply, Chris appeared and swung in between the two of them, slipping the key into the lock, and cheerfully announcing, "She will, she's with me!" He pushed open the office door and ushered her in. Before he entered, he turned to Howard and grinned as he said, "Don't worry, Mate. I'll send her back in one piece when I've finished with her." Howard smiled and nodded, wished Chris a good day too, and headed off to the corner shop.

As soon as the office door closed and Howard was out of sight, Seraphina spoke up. "Chris, what on earth was that drink you gave me in the pub? I practically passed out last night. I've got a rotten banging head this morning. I can't believe I managed to hide it from Howard all morning!"

Chris was shocked. "It was only a couple of gin and tonics, Seraphina. What a lightweight. Why didn't you tell Howard? Is he the jealous type? I do hope I haven't got you into trouble."

Unexpectedly, she felt her eyes tear up. This was not what she wanted to do. She wanted Chris to think she was a strong character built of sterner stuff. He could see she was upset and rushed to her side. He put his arm around her shoulder and gave her a little squeeze.

"Now then, young lady, what on earth is wrong? No, don't answer that yet. I'll get us both a hot drink, then you can tell me all about it."

Seraphina was surprised by his kindness. The two of them talked for the next hour about why they had moved and how she didn't understand why Howard had not got a job yet, and just how unfair it all seemed. They could have continued for hours but Seraphina remembered, just in time, that her new client would be arriving soon.

"So much for getting in early to prepare. I'll just get my face sorted before they get here."

"Don't you worry. I'll get this appointment today, Seraphina. I'll say you've been called away. Go up and work in the top office this morning, but be quiet, so that they don't know you're there." He gave her another hug, and she picked up Ziggy's shoe box and went upstairs.

****

As Howard walked down Main Street, he could see Pauline taking delivery of fresh supplies for her grocery shop. She had a cotton rag wrapped around her hand and was struggling. It looked like she had cut herself badly. "Hi Pauline, here, let me help you," he said, as he approached the shop and grabbed a large bag of carrots. "Where shall I put these?"

"You're so kind, Howard. Just inside on the left, thanks."

"There you go. What have you done to your hand? It must be bad. Look, Pauline, it's bleeding through your bandage!"

"Oh, this?" She looked at her hand and tried to readjust the bandage that she had cobbled together out of an old tea towel. "It's in such an awkward place. As soon as I go to lift anything, the damn thing opens up again. I'm sure it will be okay soon though." She tried to make light of it as if it was nothing, but he wasn't happy to leave her. He hadn't seen so much blood on a cut in a long time.

"How did you do it, Pauline?"

"Ah, well yes, now, don't criticise, will you? To be honest, I'm not sure how it happened. Something must have distracted me for just a moment. I keep a nice big knife in the shop to cut open the vegetable sacks. Anyway, one minute I was working away as normal, opening some sacks, and the next, I'd cut my hand. Right across my palm. It bled so much."

He stared at her hand. "Shouldn't you have stitches? I do hope your tetanus is up to date."

"I haven't got time for that! Who would run the shop?"

"Can't your daughter help you?"

"You're joking, aren't you? She's a teenager. She's never up early unless there's something in it for her. Take tomorrow, for example. She's got an interview in the city, so it will be Muggins here making sure she's up and at the station on time, won't it? To be honest, though, I wouldn't have it any other way. But today, you're right, she would have been handy."

Pauline let out an enormous sigh of disappointment.

Howard stayed and helped her unload the entire delivery as he wasn't the sort of person to leave someone to struggle.

As he placed the last bag of veg down and headed for the door, he said in a stern voice, "If that hand hasn't stopped bleeding the next time I see you, I'm taking you to A&E myself. Is there anything else I can help you with before I go, Pauline?"

"No, be gone with you. I'm very grateful for your help, but I can take it from here. Have yourself a great day. Bye."

Glad to have been of help, Howard continued his journey to the corner shop, where he had plans to help someone else. He wanted to be in the shop before Sarah arrived, so that he could opportunely help her again.

He wondered if he was being a silly fool and if he should be deliberately putting himself in that position. He pushed the thought to the back of his mind and convinced himself that there was no harm in it, as he sauntered casually into the shop.

"Morning, Howard. Your usual?" asked June. "And how are you this morning?" She was in a particularly chirpy mood, singing away as she prepared his latte. "You make me laugh, insisting on calling it a latte. You know it's only coffee with some frothy milk on top, don't you? You're just so 'city' sometimes," she chuckled.

Howard took his frothy coffee and had just sat down when Barbara came out from the back room with a crate of milk to restock the fridge. She was looking down and didn't see Sarah hobble in. As she turned to open the fridge, the crutches got caught in the crate and Sarah fell forward, unable to save herself.

As quick as lightning, Howard jumped up. He launched himself athletically across the shop and caught her, just in time to prevent her from falling to the floor. He held her tightly as they looked at each other in a combination of shock, surprise, and silence. It was only a few seconds, but it felt much longer for Howard.

The silence was eventually broken by June. "Sarah, your knight in shining armour seems to have come to your rescue once again!"

"Oh, err, yes, it would appear so. Although you can put me down now," she said, as Howard was still holding her. Embarrassed, he spluttered out, "Oh, I'm so sorry," and carefully helped her to her feet. "Are you okay? I didn't hurt you, did I?"

"No need to apologise. June's right. Thanks for catching me. I don't want to go breaking any more bones, do I?" She flashed a grateful smile and made his heart flutter, a feeling he had not had for many years.

Meanwhile, Barbara sat unceremoniously on the cold floor, with the milk crate in front of her and her skirt lifted embarrassingly high.

June burst out laughing and rushed over; tugging Barbara's skirt to cover her modesty before she helped her to her feet.

"You looked funny on the floor, Barbara. You almost gave everyone a flash of your knickers as you landed. I'm sorry I shouldn't laugh but look, what an achievement, you haven't smashed a single bottle. That deserves a round of applause!"

Barbara was very embarrassed and made her apologies to Sarah before scurrying off into the back again. Howard wondered if this was why they seldom saw her in the shop front. June called out, "Barbara, are you going to put this milk in the fridge then or leave it for the next customer to fall over?" Barbara came shuffling through again, apologising as she went. "I'm all of a fluster now. I'm sorry," she said, as she set about stocking up the fridge.

She was frail and bony, in her mid-fifties, and first impressions were that she was extremely shy. However, upon getting to know her, it soon became apparent that she was a notorious gossip and, once she started talking, there was no stopping her. It was also impossible to say which mood she was going to be in from one day to another.

Today, she was going for the shy option. She filled the fridge as quickly as she could and scurried out to the back again. For quite some time, Howard had wondered if Barbara even existed. June would refer to her, but he never saw her. She was either out the back, not in that day, or off sick, and he struggled to understand why June employed her. Like most of the village residents, they had been friends for years. Maybe it was that simple, he thought to himself.

Now upright, Howard and Sarah had both regained their composure. "June, one coffee to go, please," requested Sarah.

"Would you like my seat whilst you wait?" offered Howard.

"That's very kind of you, but I'm fine now. Thanks for saving me, again. That's two days in a row! You seem to be around at just the right time, don't you?"

Feeling confident, he replied, "Ha-ha, it does look that way. So what's your plan today to get to the station? You still have your coffee and crutches to deal with."

"Ah, this morning, I'm prepared. I have a plan. I've padded out my bag and made a special hole for my drink. It should be okay over my shoulder as I walk, as long as the lid goes on properly." She opened her bag to show him. He peered in and screwed up his face a little.

"I'm not sure if that's going to work. The fall seems to have upset your bag because I can't see any special hole." Thinking quickly, he continued, "Now, I wouldn't be a proper knight in shining armour if I let you hobble to the train station like that, would I? Let me help you again. I don't mind, really. And I enjoy the walk."

Sarah made a half-hearted attempt to refuse the offer, but then graciously accepted. He reminded her of someone, but she just couldn't put her finger on it. She thought maybe if she spent a little more time with him, it might jog her memory.

As they turned to leave, June looked up and winked at Howard. With a big smile on her face, she said, "You two have a lovely day now, won't you?"

As soon as the shop was empty, Barbara reappeared. "What a handsome couple those two make, don't they? Looks like they belong together. What do you think, June?"

"Now, Barbara, you mustn't talk like that. You know they're both married! Mind you, that husband of hers is proving to be a no-good so-and-so, isn't he? He should be here helping her, not leaving her to rely on the kindness of strangers."

June paused as she thought for a moment, but quickly continued, "But you know, Barbara, I can see what you mean. I never quite knew why she married Mike." She looked up and casually glanced out the shop window. "Flippin' heck, Barbara! Talk of the devil!"

The shop door opened and in marched Mike.

Barbara scurried out the back while June stood at the counter to greet him. "Hello. What can I do for you this fine morning?"

He greeted her with a sharp upward nod, then picked up a newspaper from the counter. "Just this, and my usual cigarettes."

June served him with a smile and wished him a good day. Mike hadn't heard Robbo follow him into the shop and, as he turned quickly to leave, he almost knocked him over. He offered no apology. Instead, he grunted and left the shop as quickly as he could.

"Well, he was his usual chatty self!" remarked Robbo.

"Nothing new there, then. I thought he worked nights. It's not like Mike to be up and about at this time of the day," replied June.

Robbo shrugged his shoulders and asked, "Do you think he's changed jobs, then?" As usual, he was on the lookout for the latest news or gossip.

Teasing him a little, June leaned forward and ushered him to do the same. As he got closer, she lowered her voice to a whisper. "I haven't heard of any changes down the quarry lately, not from any of my super special secret sources, anyway. What about you, Agent Robbo?"

He pulled away, half-laughing and half-scoffing. "Okay, funny. You got me again. When am I going to stop falling for this little joke of yours?"

"I know, you'd have thought you would have learnt by now. Sorry Robbo, you know I just can't resist an opportunity for a wind-up. I take it you've come for your morning paper then?"

In true June-style, she didn't wait for a reply and reached for his paper, simultaneously folding it in half with one hand and reaching for payment with the other.

"There you go." Robbo passed her the exact money and retorted, "I'll see you later, Agent June."

As soon as he had left, Barbara rushed out to the front again, like a trapdoor spider. "June, June," she said, enthusiastically. "Maybe Mike had come to help Sarah after all and is trying to catch her up." Her eyes sparkled with excitement. "I wonder how he'll feel when he finds she's already got help? You know how jealous he gets!"

Barbara didn't often say much but, once started, it was hard to stop her. She had a vivid imagination. June put it down to her reading too many books while her husband, Ian, worked nights at the local quarry.

She continued, "Ian told me the other day that Mike was thinking about switching to the day shift. He said it would mean he could keep a better eye on Sarah. Ian said they were like ships that pass in the night at the moment. He thinks Mike is obsessive about most things, including Sarah, and Ian should know. He's always telling me how Mike places everything in straight lines at work and can't stand it if things get out of order. If something goes missing, he sends an email to everyone on the site, asking for its return or else!"

June knew to let her continue until she'd talked herself out. "Oh, Barbara, Ian does seem to have a lot to say, doesn't he? I'm sure he's exaggerating." June wondered if Ian was right but didn't want to fire up her imagination further.

Ian and Mike both worked at the nearby quarry. Ian ran the processing unit whilst Mike was an engineer. They worked in separate sections and, over the years, had somehow become unlikely canteen buddies. The conversation was never much, as both liked to eat in peace. A mutual respect for privacy had developed over time and, occasionally, they shared a small piece of their lives.

In the meantime, Howard and Sarah were walking happily down to the station. He carried her bag and coffee as she hobbled along. "How long will you have the plaster on?"

"Only another three weeks and then, hopefully, I can crack on with the gardening and maybe even head back to my Zumba classes, or maybe I'm being a little ambitious for that."

"Another three weeks! That would feel like forever for me!"

Replying with a sense of sadness, she said, "I know. I was hoping if I said it quickly, it wouldn't sound too bad."

Just like the previous day, they chatted and soon arrived at the station. Howard insisted on seeing Sarah onto the train again and settled before leaving. He wished her a good day at work and suggested that he might see her again one morning. He didn't like to push his luck and made sure he promptly got off the train this time.

When he reached the top of the steps, he looked back and saw that the train was still waiting to pull away. As he turned to cross the bridge, someone jolted his shoulder backwards and he heard a rushed voice shout out, "Sorry!" The commuter guy he had seen the previous day was running for his train again and, in his rush, had clipped him with the edge of his rucksack. Howard speculated whether he would make it to the train in time.

Tempted as he was to wait and find out, he decided against it and thanked his lucky stars that that part of his life was now over.

FIVE

Thursday afternoon

Howard and Charlie followed the well-worn track that ran alongside the river, all the way to the next village and back. It was a warm sunny day and Charlie enjoyed the extra-long run. As they crossed the village on their way home, they bumped into Robbo, who was getting out of his delivery van.

"Hello," he said, as he put down his basket and knelt to stroke Charlie. The dog immediately sat down and looked lovingly at Robbo, enjoying the attention and sniffing madly at the basket. "Ah, there's nothing in there for you, Charlie. That basket's empty now. I've finished my deliveries for today."

Robbo turned his attention to Howard. "Will we see you at the local for the monthly 'Curry and Quiz' tonight, Howard? It's usually a decent event and, as I supply all the meat, the food's always excellent."

Howard smiled and replied, "I'm not sure what we're up to tonight, but I'll mention it to Seraphina when she gets home. I have heard good things about those nights, but we haven't been to one yet."

"Do try. It's usually a good turnout and lots of fun. Quite a few local characters join in, if only to show how little they know! I hope to see you later then," he replied, giving Charlie one last pat on his head before entering his shop.

It was almost lunchtime by the time Howard returned home with Charlie. He grabbed a sandwich and took it through to his study. He knew he was supposed to be looking for a job, but he had other ideas.

Unbeknown to Seraphina, he had been keeping himself busy by writing a novel. For years, he had promised himself that he would write a fast-paced story about high finance, risky deals, controversy, shock, and deceit. It was an area in which he felt well-versed, having spent his entire working life in that environment. As it was a new venture, he wanted to write the book before he told her. Plus, being a novice writer, he wasn't ready for any feedback, no matter how constructive it might be. Sadly, Seraphina assumed he was wasting time on his laptop, writing in, what she often referred to lately as, 'his stupid diary'.

He finished his sandwich and settled down to spend the afternoon writing. Time ticked by quickly as he tapped away on the keyboard until Seraphina interrupted him. "Hi, I'm home. Howard, where are you?"

For a moment, he thought she must have finished early. He checked the huge round clock that sat directly above the fireplace in the study. It was 5:45 pm already, and he hadn't even prepared tea. She would not be happy. "Hello, Gorgeous. I'm just coming," he called out.

He quickly saved his work, closed the document, and headed down the hallway to join her in the kitchen. He watched her place her designer handbag on the marbled kitchen surface and take off her coat.

She glanced around the immaculate new kitchen and noticed something was obviously lacking. She couldn't help herself. "You haven't cooked any dinner, have you? What have you been doing all day whilst I've been at work?"

She paused briefly, but silence greeted the opportunity to reply. "No, I didn't think so."

Just then, Howard remembered about the curry night at the pub. It might be my 'get-out-of-jail-free' card, he thought. "Hold on a minute will you, and give me a chance to speak. Robbo was telling me about the monthly 'Curry and Quiz' night at the Coach and Horses. I thought it would be nice to go. He was quite enthusiastic about it, and it's an opportunity to support the local pub. What do you say?"

He could see that she was thinking and it surprised him when she replied, "Hmm, well, I guess that's a 'yes' then, as there's nothing ready here. Okay, let's go." A smirk appeared on her face as she continued, "You never know what the night might hold!"

Suspicious of her optimistic tones, he asked, "What does that mean?"

"Well, you never know. You might walk away with a job, just like I did!" she said, raising her eyebrows at him. "Right then, what time does this thing start?"

Feeling somewhat squashed by her reply, he answered, "Actually, I'm not sure. I'll ring the pub now and find out." After a quick chat with Debbie, he had all the information he needed.

"It's lucky I rang. They were full, but Debbie said they've just had two cancellations, so we're okay. It must be good if it sells out. Food is served at 6:30 pm and the quiz starts soon afterwards, so it won't be a late night."

They spent the next ten minutes hurriedly getting ready. Fortunately, getting anywhere in the village never took long, and they made it to the pub with ten minutes to spare. It was already quite busy, so they headed straight to the bar. As they waited, a familiar voice shouted over. "Seraphina, Howard, how fabulous. I didn't know you were coming to the quiz tonight!"

Chris tapped the seats next to him with enthusiasm and said, "Here, come and join me. You can help make up my team of four." He was sitting at his favourite table in the corner. It had a good view of the entire pub and had bench seats on two sides, which were handy for getting more people around the table.

"Shall we?" Seraphina asked Howard. He looked over to see if Chris needed a drink, but he was happily sipping an almost full pint. He noticed that he also had a clipboard with a pen attached to a piece of string and wondered if he was a professional pub quizzer. He had heard of people like that.

Waving to Chris, Howard gave him a thumbs-up as they waited at the bar. Debbie quickly greeted them and sorted their drinks and food order. Loaded with drinks, cutlery, quiz sheets, and pens, they walked over to join Chris. "You didn't mention you were coming here tonight either. Have you come straight from work?" Seraphina asked as she placed her drink on the table.

"Ah, there's still so much about me you have to learn, my dear Seraphina," Chris said, smiling. "Anyway, it's more of a surprise to see the two of you here! A pleasant surprise, obviously. It's always nice to see the two of you out and about." He stood up and pulled out a chair for

Seraphina, whilst simultaneously ushering Howard towards the other chair.

"Here, sit down, both of you. No need to stand on parade. So, Howard, tell me, how have you settled in now all the building work is done?"

"Oh, yes, it's great. Thanks for asking. We're very pleased with how it's all turned out. Aren't we, Seraphina?" Howard tried to pull her back into the conversation as, unusually, she suddenly appeared distracted. She kept looking around the pub to see who was there, and wasn't listening when she answered, "Yes, I haven't been to the quiz before." Howard looked at Seraphina with a confused expression and asked, "What are you on about, Darling? Chris asked if we'd settled into the house now that we're free of builders."

He tried to make light of her obvious lack of attention and jovially replied, "I don't know where her head is half the time, you know. I hope she pays more attention than this when she's at work! Anyway, Chris, this should be a good night. We haven't been to the local for a while, have we Seraphina?"

She smiled and nodded in agreement. "No, Howard, we haven't, have we?" She turned and looked at Chris with wide eyes and raised eyebrows, silently pleading with him not to mention yesterday's after-work drinks.

Howard continued, "Chris, you haven't told us who makes up the fourth member of this team, have you? Anyone we know?" Chris stood up, and replied, "I'm sure my team member will be here very soon. I know you're going to get along just fine. In the meantime, I'm off to the bar to get another pint in before the curry arrives. Do either of you care for another?"

"We're fine, thanks," Howard answered promptly for the two of them.

As Chris went to the bar, a tall, well-dressed man with neatly gelled-back dark wavy hair appeared and took a seat at Chris's table. As he smoothly slid along the padded bench, he winked at Seraphina before stretching out his hand towards her husband. Howard was shaking hands with the stranger before he even realised it.

"Well, good evening. Would I be right in assuming I have the pleasure of making the acquaintance of Mr Seraphina? How very nice to meet you." Still holding his hand, Howard replied, "Um, yes, I suppose I am."

He looked at Seraphina with wide eyes but she didn't return his stare. She couldn't take her eyes off the tall, dark, and unexpectedly handsome Mr Palmer, who was sitting directly in front of her. He had gelled down his wild curly hair and cleaned himself up. She thought he looked remarkably slick, especially with his neatly trimmed stubble beard.

Eventually, she dragged her eyes away and explained to Howard, "This is Mr Palmer. He's a customer of ours and also a good friend of Chris's. He brought his accounts into the office yesterday."

Seraphina's stomach was doing somersaults, as was her head. She could not believe her eyes. The transformation was amazing. Yesterday he was such a tramp. She knew she had to keep her cool.

Ziggy smiled broadly at Seraphina and put his elbows on the table. "Now then, there's no need to be so formal, is there? Any employee of Chris's is a friend of mine. Well, I know that's not quite how it goes, but who cares? Can I get you and Mr Seraphina a drink?"

She suddenly realised she had not introduced him properly. "Sorry, this is my husband, Howard, and no thanks, we're good for drinks. We've not long got ours but thank you anyway. Howard suggested we try the 'Curry and Quiz' night and so, well, here we are."

"Howard, terrific to meet you, and good to know that great minds think alike. Chris told me he had a new team member a few weeks ago, what with the old bag retiring. Oops, did I say that out loud?" He looked around the pub in an exaggerated theatrical manner, followed by a loud belly laugh.

"Who am I kidding? Like I care. She was sooooo boring. Your wife Seraphina is a much better addition to the business, I'm sure. I can hardly believe I only met your lovely wife this week, but then I have been a tad busy lately with my work. Now Howard, call me Ziggy. Everyone else does. But, first things first, I'm off to the bar to get a drink before the food turns up." He stood up with the same enthusiasm that he had sat down with and joined Chris at the bar.

Howard turned sharply to Seraphina and asked, "Is this the man you described to me as a tramp? Do you take me for some kind of idiot? Let's be clear now. Is this the same guy you told me about yesterday, the one who had his accounts in the shoe box? Well?"

He stared at Seraphina, waiting for a decent explanation.

"Yes, yes, it is," she stuttered. "He didn't look like that at all. Honestly, he really did look like a tramp yesterday. I couldn't believe my eyes either!" Before they could discuss Ziggy any further, Chris returned to the table.

"Hi, I'm back. It's chaos at the bar now because the food's on its way. This is such a popular night, you know. I can't believe you've not been before," he said, as he placed two fresh pints of pale ale on the table.

"Look out, you lot, here comes the grub," called Debbie, as she arrived with the food.

"Looks like I got back just in the nick of time. I'm looking forward to this. Thanks, Debbie. I'm really quite hungry now," Chris said enthusiastically.

"Here you go, lamb curry it is." Debbie placed two large plates of curry in the middle of the table. Then another with poppadums and a little stainless-steel tub of mango chutney. "I'll be back with the rest in a jiffy," she said, as she dashed back to the bar.

"That looks exceedingly good," said Chris, as he unwrapped his knife and fork. As he reached for the plates, Debbie returned.

"Oh, Chris, not so fast. I've got yours here. You wanted chicken, didn't you?" She put another two plates on the table.

"So, do we assume Ziggy makes up the fourth player, then?" asked Seraphina.

Chris didn't need to answer. At the sight of the food arriving, Ziggy repeated his earlier manoeuvre. He slid along the bench seat while simultaneously unwrapping his knife and fork from its tissue sleeping bag and arrived seated upright, ready to eat.

"Ah, yes. I saw you three chatting from the bar. I thought Ziggy had explained he was the fourth man. We've been quizzing partners for years, haven't we Ziggy?" explained Chris.

"And a few more things besides," replied Ziggy, as he took a sip of his drink. He looked at Chris like he was peering over the top of imaginary glasses before his face broke into a cheeky grin and he continued, "We've done some crazy things over the years but hey, that's all part of life, isn't it?"

Just as Robbo had described, it was a popular night and everyone was in the pub that evening. June was there with Barbara, Ian and their daughter, Cassie, to make up a team of four. Pauline turned up with a group of girlfriends, and there were another couple of teams still in their cricket whites. The cricket team made sure they planned their practice evenings around curry nights and had come straight off the green. By the end of the quiz, the cricket lads were a little rowdy but in good spirits.

Everyone enjoyed their meals, just as Robbo had predicted, and Chris and Ziggy demonstrated remarkable general knowledge throughout the quiz. So much so, that Seraphina hoped they were in with a chance of winning.

Debbie had just said the mandatory public 'Thank you' to Robbo for supplying the meat, and silence fell as she was about to announce the quiz winners. "And the winning team is …"

She paused long enough for the first shout-out from the crowd of, "Get on with it, it's not X Factor you know," which was followed by a round of laughter.

"Right then, ladies and gentlemen. Now I have your attention, I can tell you that it was a close call this evening, but tonight's winning team is June's Jivers. Give them a big round of applause, will you? And thanks for taking part."

The crown cheered and clapped together with a few calls of 'fixed' and 'cheats' and 'just wait till next month'.

Seraphina looked shocked when she heard the comments and Ziggy noticed her frowning.

"Don't you worry about the jeering, my dear," said Ziggy. "It's all good wholesome fun and, to be honest, they're pretty mild this month; probably because it was June's team. Everyone loves June."

A quick chime on the pub bell and, once again, Debbie had everyone's attention. "Now then, you horrible lot. Don't forget the prize is a free meal to the winning team next time." She did a quick scan of the pub and called out, "Come on, Robbo, where are you hiding? Show yourself and tell the lovely girls and boys what we're going to have next time, can you?"

Robbo stood up and made himself known, as he casually waved his hand in the air. Everyone called out meal suggestions. "Lamb stew," said one voice and T-Bone steak was another cheeky suggestion.

"Good effort," Robbo shouted out. "But the clue's in the title. It's a curry night. I plan on providing beef next time." He declared this proudly and lapped up the attention when everyone cheered.

As Debbie began to speak, they all quietened down.

"Right then, ladies and gents. Don't forget to put your name down if you're coming next month, so we can make sure there's enough to go around and thanks, as always, for continuing to make this monthly event such a success."

Quietly Seraphina said to Howard, "It's getting late now. I'm just going to nip to the ladies, and then we should think about making a move." She left the table and made her way across the pub. As she returned, she could hear raised voices and hoped it wasn't trouble but, as she got closer, she could see that it was Spencer, the cricket team captain; and he was shouting at Howard.

"I don't cut and roll that green for my health you know, Mister! You city folk make me sick. You come buying up our property and taking our jobs. You've got no respect for our country ways!"

Howard was usually slow to anger but tonight he too had enjoyed more drinks than usual. He stood up and, in a clear and slightly raised voice, he replied, "Now look, I'm sorry for walking over your hallowed green yesterday and I won't do it again, but there's certainly no need to be rude."

Seraphina reached over to get her coat but, as she moved, she caught Spencer's eye. He took a deep breath and turned his attention to her. "And as for you, you can't seem to stay out of this place, can you?"

Seraphina turned around quickly. She looked first at Spencer and then at Howard, whose eyebrows were raised. He was about to speak but Chris got there first. He raised his voice initially but got quieter and quieter as he spoke.

"Now, that's quite enough, Spencer. You can stop right there. I asked Seraphina here for a quick celebratory drink after work, not that it's any business of yours. So, what exactly are you saying then, Spence? Someone that moves to the village, buys a house, employs local tradespeople to work on that house but then isn't allowed to come to the local pub! Is that what you mean? Let's be clear here, Spence. What exactly is it you're trying to say?"

Seraphina was impressed and relieved that Chris had cut in as he dealt with the confrontation calmly and logically. He lent closer and closer to Spencer and his voice got quieter and quieter until they were face to face. He spoke just loudly enough so that only Spencer and the people immediately next to him could hear him say, "Grow up and get over yourself. It's not all about tradition and your flippin' cricket team. Tradition is that things change!"

Spencer reared up, lifted his right arm, and tried to throw a punch but got dragged back to his seat by his fellow cricketers, accompanied by the usual calls of, "Leave it, Spence" and "Come on you, not causing trouble again."

Meanwhile, Howard was astounded. He knew nothing of Seraphina's visit to the pub and wanted to know what was going on. "So Seraphina, when was this drink then? It seems your presence in the pub has only gone unnoticed by me, and I live with you!"

Just then, Sarah's husband came barging into the pub, shouting out, "Where's Howard?" "Bloody hell, Howard. I hope he doesn't mean you!" said Seraphina.

But he did!

After knocking a couple of locals out of the way, Mike marched straight up to Howard, grabbed him by his jacket lapels, and pushed him against the wall.

"Stay away from my wife. She can look after herself!"

Ziggy was quick off the mark. His height and strength were exceptional assets as he jumped up and dragged Mike off Howard. His feet skimmed the ground as Ziggy carried him out of the pub unaided and, for a moment, the pub fell silent.

Neither Howard nor Seraphina knew where to look. After what seemed like an age, Debbie broke the silence as she shouted out, "Come on then, you awful lot. Last orders, thank you, before I change my mind." She rang the bell above the bar, extra loudly, one last time.

Ziggy returned and announced that Mike had been drinking heavily since the end of the cricket game and he had packed him off home.

Chris continued, "Don't you two worry about him. He's very protective of his wife, Sarah. If he's not having a go at you, he's having a go at someone else. It's just your turn. I guess you must have spoken to her at some point, Howard. Here, let's walk these two troublemakers home, shall we, Ziggy?"

Ziggy laughed loudly, saying, "If you ask me, you're both going to fit in here nicely, judging by your performances this evening. It's been great fun, hasn't it, Chris?"

Howard and Seraphina couldn't apologise or thank Chris and Ziggy enough. As they walked home together, Chris commented, "Don't worry about it. You might have been this evening's end-of-night entertainment and be the talk of the village for a couple of days, but you'll soon be yesterday's news. Won't they, Ziggy?"

"Oh, yes, for sure, my darling newest friends," said Ziggy, as he launched himself between Howard and Seraphina, resting an arm over each of their shoulders. "As soon as the next exciting thing happens, or some new gossip comes along, you'll sadly be forgotten."

Chris picked up the conversation. "Anyway, you're nobody until you've caused a scene in the pub. Just consider it a kind of initiation ceremony."

While they roared with laughter, Seraphina and Howard didn't. They glanced at each other in silence.

As they approached their house, a relieved Howard announced, "This is us and, thanks again, Ziggy."

"No worries. Being extra tall has its advantages sometimes."

"I'll see you tomorrow," Seraphina said to Chris. She smiled at Ziggy as she unlocked the front door and added, "Unless you two would like to come in for a coffee?"

"We'd better not," said Chris. "Although I would love to see how the house has turned out, it's getting late and it's a school night. Another time would be lovely, though."

"Same here," said Ziggy, laughing. "Well, only if I'm invited of course, and because I'm nosey, but I'd better push off now."

Seraphina was still trying to work out the tramp-to-riches transformation as Ziggy shook Howard's hand and kissed her on the cheek.

After all the pleasant goodbyes on the doorstep, once they were inside, there was a stone-cold silence between them. Who was going to speak first? Seraphina wanted to know who Sarah was. Howard wondered why he knew nothing about Seraphina's trip to the pub after work.

Eventually, Howard broke the silence. "I think we need to talk, but not tonight. It's late and I want to go to bed. I suggest we talk about this tomorrow evening, okay?"

Seraphina had so many thoughts whizzing through her head but she agreed.

They were soon in bed and settling down for the night. Almost asleep, Seraphina heard a scream, some muffled shouting, and a car door being slammed.

"Well, that just about finishes off the evening, doesn't it? Goodnight."

"Goodnight," said Howard, deciding it was best to leave his diary that evening.

SIX

Friday early morning

Seraphina and Howard had a restless night, both tossing and turning. When the alarm went off, they struggled to find the energy to face the day. Exhausted and concerned about the state of their relationship, Seraphina rolled over and looked at Howard. "Are we okay?" she asked.

Howard had spent most of the night worrying. He was desperate for their new life to be perfect but, at the moment, it seemed far from it. He tried to sound positive. "Of course we are. Look, why don't we forget about last night for now and talk about it later this evening over a takeaway?"

"If you like," she replied, as she leaned into him and gave him a hug. Her actions said it all, and he knew instantly that they would be okay. They just had to talk it out.

"Come on now, you don't want to be late for work today. Charlie and I can walk with you, if you like."

Seraphina accepted with a thankful smile. "That would be nice."

As usual, Howard was ready first. Heading for the stairs, he asked, "Egg and bacon, or cereal and toast?"

"I'll just have some toast today, please."

Despite the events of the previous night, he skipped down the stairs with a spring in his step. They would talk things through later and hopefully, it would be a kind of reset.

He laid a place setting for each of them at the breakfast bar and made two coffees. Just as he pushed down the lever on the toaster, Seraphina appeared.

"This looks nice, thanks," she said, lifting herself onto a stool. "I was thinking in the shower that perhaps we could do something nice this weekend. Maybe a trip to London for a show or some shopping. We haven't done that in ages, have we?"

"That sounds like a great idea. I'll look for some inspiration today, and we can decide this evening, if you like."

"Or we could have dinner and a film? Anything to break the monotony we've got ourselves into recently. Do you agree?" She was chatty this morning. It was the most they had spoken to each other in the morning for weeks.

"That sounds perfect."

Howard chased Charlie through to the hallway to put his lead on, and called back, "Come on Seraphina, have you got everything? It's about time we made a move."

"I'm coming, I'm coming," she called and dashed to catch up.

As Howard opened the front door and pulled back on Charlie's lead he said, "Blimey, he's full of energy this morning. I thought he'd got past all this tugging! Anyway, are there any shows you've been wanting to see lately?"

"I know!" she declared with an air of excitement in her voice. "Instead of a show, why don't we go to Kew Gardens? Now the house is done, we can think about the garden. It might give us some inspiration, and it would make a wonderful day out. What do you think?"

"That's a great idea. Wow, we're here already. I guess that's a benefit of working locally. There's no long commute anymore. I feel like Charlie pulled me all the way. I wonder if dogs are allowed in Kew Gardens. He could burn off some of this energy."

Smiling at Seraphina, he continued, "I'll see you tonight then. Oh, and while I think about it, do you have any preference for the takeaway?"

Any other day she would have responded with a spikey comeback to his commuting comment but, this morning, she just let it go, and replied, "Surprise me. It doesn't have to be a takeaway. Whatever's easier for you! Have a lovely day and I'll see you tonight." She even gave him a quick peck on the cheek, something she hadn't done for ages.

When she walked into the office, she was surprised to see Chris already sitting at his desk, as she usually arrived first. He greeted her with a wide smile and asked cheerfully, as he stood up, "I'm making, do you want a drink?"

"Yes please, I'll have one of those latte coffee pod things, if there's any left."

She sat down at her desk and went through her usual morning routine. She switched on her PC and reached into her drawer for her pen and wondered why he was in so early. Slowly, the events of last night replayed through her head. Suddenly, she wondered if he was angry with her and if she had jeopardised her job.

He quickly pulled her out of her thoughts though and made her jump, by asking, "How were things for you when you got home? I hope you weren't in too much trouble!"

"That's kind of you to ask. I'm so embarrassed. I knew I should have told him I'd been to the pub with you. I didn't mean to keep it from him. It just kind of went that way, but you know that, don't you?"

Chris nodded and gave a reassuring smile as he pulled a chair up to her desk and passed her the drink.

"Thank you. We agreed last night probably wasn't the best time to talk, so we're going to discuss things tonight. I am sorry, Chris. I didn't mean to put you in an awkward situation, and you even covered for me!" She could feel herself getting hot and flustered. As she spoke, she thought the worst. "I understand if you feel the need to sack me. It doesn't look good for your company, does it? I'm so sorry."

"Why on earth do you think I would sack you? We're not in the 1960s anymore!" said Chris, laughing at the suggestion. "Don't you worry. It's probably the most exciting bit of action this village has seen since Spencer's wife went off with the vicar's daughter! I'm sure everything will work out okay. Let's get some work done, and I'll tell you more about Spencer's ex-wife over lunch."

Seraphina was relieved. Her emotions were all over the place and she put it down to the lack of sleep. With a busy day ahead of her, she took a deep breath and focused her attention on her work.

Throughout the morning, the sight of Ziggy's shoe box distracted her. A fleeting infatuation, or what? Annoyed with herself, she stood up and placed it on top of the filing cabinet behind her. Out of sight out of mind she hoped, and told herself that his accounts could wait until later.

As the morning turned into early afternoon, her stomach grumbled. Glancing at the clock, she saw that it was lunchtime. Heading to the kitchenette area, Chris joined her. As promised, whilst they sat eating their sandwiches, he told her about Spencer's ex-wife. She listened intently, nodding and asking questions. She was grateful for the distraction and the chance to talk about something other than her own problems.

After lunch, she felt re-energised and ready to tackle the rest of her tasks for the day. She was determined to finish her existing case, so she could start on the infamous shoe box.

****

Meanwhile, Howard mulled over the previous night's events as he walked Charlie. He wondered why Spencer had been so nasty to Seraphina, and how he was going to explain to her why Mike was so adamant that he should stay away from Sarah. He would have to explain everything.

He walked some more, with Charlie leading the way, and eventually concluded that he hadn't done anything wrong. He told himself he was only helping a fellow human being, and he had been in the right place at the right time. Well, sort of. He decided that a little poetic licence wouldn't hurt, and it might even help.

When Howard arrived at the shop, he was much later than usual. He could hear June and Barbara deep in conversation as he tied Charlie up outside.

"Morning, June. My usual, please. I've got Charlie with me this morning, so I'll take the table out front. I don't like to leave him outside by himself. Is that okay?"

"Ah ha, here he is, Barbara. We thought we might not see you this morning. We wondered if you were going to lie low after last night's shenanigans!" June laughed, but then instantly saw a look of concern wash over his face. She quickly continued, "Don't you worry about it, my love. While the village is talking about you, they're leaving someone else alone."

"To be honest, I hadn't given it any thought. Are we likely to be the talk of the village?" He was surprised by June's comment since he hadn't talked to Seraphina about the previous night, yet everyone else already had an opinion.

"As you weren't in at your normal time, we didn't think we were going to see you this morning. Even Sarah asked after you. We wondered if you might have waited for her at the station, rather than walk her there again. Barbara even suggested you might be there already."

Howard was shocked and raised his voice saying, "Why on earth would you think that? I only helped her to the train a couple of times and, after Mike's specific request last night, it's highly unlikely that I'll be doing it again!"

He was angry. Maybe Seraphina was right, and they had moved to Smallsville.

June, visibly taken aback by his comments, replied apologetically, "Oh, I'm ever so sorry, Howard. Look, I'll bring your latte out to you as soon as it's ready." She loved to be involved in things but realised, on this occasion, that she had overstepped the mark big time.

Almost slamming his money down on the counter, Howard didn't wait for his change. He took his paper and went outside to sit at the small, round café table. He made a fuss of Charlie and told him, "What a good boy you are. You don't gossip, do you?"

He flicked through his paper and was in half-a-mind to forego the coffee and head home, when a police car went by at speed, with its siren blaring. It was an unusual sight for their quiet village, especially as an ambulance was following it. His curiosity was piqued. He was used to seeing ambulances, but it was unusual to see two emergency vehicles together.

Charlie didn't like it at all and started barking loudly. It took a while to calm him down, which was not helped by the sudden flow of talkative people walking past.

Whatever was going on that morning was delaying Howard's latte. He looked over his shoulder into the shop to see that a queue had formed. Not being in a rush, he decided to wait. June would surely be out in a minute.

As he turned over the last page of his newspaper, there was still no latte. He decided to chase it up, as the queue had cleared. As he walked in, he asked, "What's a guy got to do to get a drink in this place?"

June looked up. "Oh my, I am sorry. I completely forgot you were sitting out there, waiting. We've just had such a rush because the police have closed the train station! You'll never guess why!" True to form, she didn't wait for the answer and leaned into Howard, announcing conspiratorially, "It seems there's been a stabbing at the train station this morning!"

The news shook Howard. If he still lived in the city, he wouldn't have given it a second thought, but in the village, it was most unexpected. "Really? That's terrible. Do you know who?"

June shook her head and answered, "No, but I understand the police have cordoned off the train station and they're there now, investigating. From what my customers were saying, it sounds like the man was in a serious condition. I heard several customers say he was dead but I'm sure they were just exaggerating!" She paused for a moment, then said, "I think I'll make myself a coffee and join you, Howard, if you don't mind."

He could see that the news had shaken her badly.

"Barbara, nip out the back will you, and grab that bottle of whisky I keep in the cabinet next to the dining room door. I think we all need a little something extra in our coffee this morning. I feel a bit unsettled and I'm going to close the shop for a while, so that I can regain my composure." She looked up and saw Charlie sitting patiently outside.

"You can't leave Charlie out there, Howard. Bring him in and let him sit in the house for a while." She was still feeling guilty for gossiping about him earlier and forgetting his latte.

"If you're sure? That's very kind of you."

Charlie loved having somewhere new to sniff and explore, and he quickly found a blanket on June's sofa to curl up on. She glanced over at him. Surprised, she announced, "Good Lord. That's exactly where my old dog used to snuggle." She paused for a moment before adding, "It seems strange to see a dog there again. My little darling, Freddy, has been gone a long time now."

"Come on, Charlie. Off that sofa. That's no place for dogs," scolded Howard.

But June didn't mind. "Don't you worry about Charlie. If he's comfortable, he can stay there."

She turned the sign on the shop door to read 'Closed' and took a seat at the round table. Barbara arrived with three coffees and a bottle of whisky. "I'll be Mum, shall I?" she offered, topping all the cups up with a generous shot.

"Are you two all right now?" Howard enquired, his previous annoyance forgotten.

June nodded and said, "Yes, it's quite unsettling, isn't it, when you stop to think about it? I've always felt safe in a small village like this, but I guess these things can happen anywhere."

Barbara, who had been quiet until then, added, "It sure is a shock to the system. We're just not used to this sort of thing here."

Howard sipped his coffee, with its warm kick of whisky. "Do you think they'll catch who did it?"

June shrugged her shoulders. "I don't know. I hope so. It's a small community and everyone knows each other, so it's hard to imagine someone getting away with it, without being seen."

Barbara chipped in, "Well, you'd think so, wouldn't you? But from what I overheard, no one knew the guy on the platform. I heard one say they were used to seeing him at the station every day, but that was all. Maybe he was a bit of a loner. I heard someone else describe him. Apparently, he was a middle-aged man with short brown hair, a beard, and a blue jacket."

Taking a deep breath, she continued, "Well, we didn't see Sarah come back, so she must have been on the train before it happened. At least she'll make it to work today. We'll just have to be patient and let the police do their job."

June hissed at Barbara, "After last night and what Howard said earlier, I'm surprised you've even mentioned

Sarah again. I thought she was 'persona non grata' and not to be mentioned again! Don't you have a filter, Barbara?"

"Oh, I'm sorry. It was only because of the station thing that I thought of her, honest," Barbara replied apologetically.

They looked at each other and turned to Howard, who laughingly said, "I'm sorry I was grumpy with you earlier. It's moments like these that give you a reality check."

Relieved at his attitude, June replied, "Don't give it a second thought, my dear."

For a few minutes, they all sat in silence, each lost in their thoughts as they sipped their whisky-laced coffee. Charlie, sensing the mood, got up from his spot on the sofa and joined them. He nuzzled his head under Howard's hand. Comforted by his presence and grateful to own a dog, Howard stroked him lovingly. "At least we have you, eh boy, if there's a murderer on the loose."

June and Barbara looked at each other and both called out simultaneously, "Murderer?" June continued, "I don't think he's dead! No one actually said he was, just that it didn't look good."

Howard replied quickly, realising he had worried the ladies, "Oh, I'm sorry. I guess that's what living in a city does. It's made me assume the worst all the time. Sorry. And obviously, fingers crossed. I hope he's okay."

While Charlie took the chance to sneak quietly back to the comfort of the sofa, June decided she would try to lighten the mood, by saying, "So, Howard, are you doing anything special this weekend?"

"Seraphina and I were just discussing that this morning. Tomorrow, we plan to visit Kew Gardens. Funny really. Despite last night's events, we haven't had a falling out."

Feeling the effects of the embellished coffee, and realising his tongue was about to run away with him, he decided it was a good time to leave.

"June, how do you feel now? And you, Barbara, are you fit to reopen?"

June replied, "Oh I'm fine now, my love. I guess it was all a bit of a shock, but we should get on."

Barbara spoke up, and said, "I can't believe someone would do something like that. I mean, I've heard of break-ins or stabbings in other towns and cities, but not in our village!"

June nodded in agreement. "It's a cruel world we live in, but we can't let fear rule our lives. We have to carry on, my dear."

Barbara smiled at her friend, before saying, "You're right June. We'll be okay. We have each other."

June stood up and stretched her arms. "Well, let's get to work then. We have a shop to run."

Between them, the women cleared the table and put away the coffee cups.

"Right, I'm off home then, to sort out our day trip," said Howard, as he rolled up his well-thumbed paper and headed for the door. Pointing at the closed sign on his way, he asked, "Do you want me to turn this to 'Open'?"

"Yes please," called out June. "Enjoy the rest of your day, won't you?"

SEVEN

Friday mid-morning

When Howard got home, he fired up the laptop in the study and began researching Kew Gardens, trying to find the best route to take. Researching information about dogs on trains, he suddenly realised that he had forgotten Charlie. Blaming June's whisky-laced coffee, he quickly grabbed his jacket and rushed out to fetch him.

As he hurried to the shop, he was so preoccupied with thoughts of his dog that he almost walked into a crowd of ladies waiting outside the grocers. He looked up and noticed it was closed. Maybe Pauline had taken herself to A&E after all, he wondered, as he rushed by. He flew into the shop so quickly that he startled June.

"June, June, I'm so sorry. I can't believe I forgot Charlie. It must have been that whisky and all the commotion earlier. It completely threw me."

"Slow down there, Howard. No harm done. I wondered how long it would take you to realise. Charlie has been such a good boy. He's quite a friendly chappy, isn't he? We've been getting along nicely. If ever you want to leave him in good hands, I'd be delighted to take care of him. I haven't had a dog around the house for years now. Not since my Freddy passed away, bless his soul."

Just as June finished speaking, Pauline walked into the shop, looking visibly flustered. "Bless his soul indeed. He didn't make it, you know. It was terrible and the police are treating it as murder!"

June's expression turned grave, confused by Pauline's statement. "Murder? What? The man at the station?"

Pauline replied, "It was me. I sat with the man at the station! I was seeing my daughter off for her interview today and making sure she got on the right train. I think I mentioned it to you yesterday, Howard. Well, I've only just been allowed to leave the train station."

She was in shock and having trouble making sense. Approaching her with a gentle touch, June said, "You poor thing, come and sit down over here. You must be all of a tither. Barbara will bring us all a nice cup of sweet tea."

Pauline gratefully accepted June's offer and sat down. "How kind, June. I do feel a little shaky. A nice cup of tea would be lovely."

June turned to Barbara, saying, "Can you be an absolute darling and make a pot of tea for all of us, a little like before? Please."

Barbara went to make the tea, as Howard and June sat down next to Pauline.

Howard asked, "Do you know what happened? We heard about a stabbing at the train station, but you said murder."

Pauline took a deep breath and began, "Well, I was on the platform and I'd just waved goodbye to Kay. I turned to leave when this man was standing next to me, holding his side as if in pain, staring right at me. He appeared from nowhere and, before I could ask if he needed any help, he suddenly collapsed."

Howard and June were all ears, listening intently to Pauline's every word, while Barbara lent forward over the counter as she strained to listen over the sound of the boiling kettle.

"Oh, Pauline, I'm so sorry," said June. "It must have been traumatic for you."

Pauline replied, "It was lucky that Kay couldn't see anything from the train, thank goodness. She's already got enough on her plate with the interview today."

"You know, Pauline," said June, "the shop will have to wait today. This is not a normal day at all!" She got up and walked quickly over to the door, flicked the sign to 'Closed' again and threw over the bolt. Barbara was quick to arrive with a tray full of steaming cups of sweet tea and handed them out. Howard wondered if she had put a little something extra in Pauline's cup, like earlier.

Pauline took a sip of the tea and said, "Thank you. That's lovely." She wrapped her hands around the delicate bone china cup as if she was warming her hands in the middle of winter.

"When we heard the news earlier about a stabbing, I closed the shop for a while, didn't I Howard?" said June, glancing at him for agreement. "Howard even went home forgetting his dog. He's just come back for Charlie now. That's what shock does to you!"

Howard joined in, trying to lighten the mood a little. "I know, I'm never going to get away from this place today, am I? So, Pauline, are you okay now?"

June repeated Howard's words. "Yes, how are you feeling now, my dear?" Howard realised this was June's way of saying, 'Tell me everything you can', so he sat back in his chair and made himself comfy.

"Thank you. I think I'm feeling a little better now. I didn't realise how popular the early morning train was. I suppose it's because I never catch it."

June continued to pry. "Yes and, lucky me, I catch all the passing trade. But never mind that, Dear. What makes you say it's murder if the man only collapsed?"

Pauline tried to summarise. "Oh, yes, I forgot to say. So, I waved goodbye to Kay, turned to leave, and saw this chap holding his side. He collapsed on the platform right next to me. I knelt to see if I could help. I thought maybe he was having a heart attack or something. Then I saw it! He had a large knife sticking out his side!"

June gasped in shock. "It must have been awful for you, dear." Keen to get as much detail as possible, she continued with her questions. "Did you recognise the poor man?"

"Yes, I did, June, and yes, it was awful. Once the blood started coming, it just wouldn't stop. It just seemed to pump out of him. I shouted for help and one of the station staff appeared, took one look and called 999. I was trying to comfort him but, apart from holding his hand, there was little I could do."

As she spoke, she got faster and faster. "I could see him getting weaker as the pool of blood got bigger. All I could think of was at least he wasn't lying on the cold concrete slab, as his rucksack had broken his fall. I put my handbag under his head for comfort. It was surreal, like a dream. I can't believe it." She was clearly shaken as she recalled the events of her morning.

"That's terrible, Pauline," sympathised June.

"And even worse for the chap!" chipped in Barbara, whose comment was greeted by raised eyebrows from both Howard and June.

"Gosh, poor you," continued June. "My mind is doing somersaults now, so it must have been awful for you! You said you knew him? What about his family?"

"Yes, I recognised him. He'd occasionally been in my shop, but I'd not seen him out and about. I just knew him as Andy. Oh June, you're right, his poor family. I hope he didn't have any children."

Pauline looked up at Howard and her voice trembled. "He was about your age, Howard, and your kind of build. He didn't seem in much pain. He just lay on the platform, not moving. He kept drifting in and out of sleep whilst I held his hand and waited for the ambulance. It's silly, but I've seen in films where they always want the person to stay awake, so I just kept talking to him."

She composed herself and took another sip of tea. "I think he was losing too much blood. You should have seen the look on his face. He looked very confused."

June took Pauline's hand and gave it a squeeze to comfort her and, with that, she burst into tears. "Oh dear, look at me. I don't know why I'm crying. I didn't even know him," she said, as she reached into her pocket for a tissue.

June reassured her by saying, "Now, don't you fret, my dear. It will be the shock. You're amongst friends here now. Shall I slip something a little stronger in that teacup? We all did earlier." In her usual style, she didn't wait for an answer and beckoned Barbara off in the general direction of the whisky, "You know where it is, don't you, Barbara?"

Barbara returned swiftly and offered, "Shall I be Mum?" as she held the now-familiar bottle of whisky.

"Just this once then," replied June, and Barbara began another round of shots in everyone's tea. Howard was going to say no but, before he could, she had topped his cup up. It was turning into quite a boozy morning.

Pauline took a sip before she declared, "Blimey Barbara. That's strong!" But it seemed to do the job, as she regained her composure.

"I don't think I'll ever forget the look on his face as the paramedics carried him off on the stretcher. He just looked confused. As they took him away, his eyes closed. They seemed to work on him for ages in the ambulance. I was just straightening myself out when a nice policeman came up to me and asked if I could give them a statement straightaway. Then he gave me his card, saying something about if I needed to, I could contact him again. Can you believe it? I never knew the police had business cards."

Pauline rummaged in her pocket. After pulling out several tissues, some string, and a couple of large red elastic bands, she found the card. "Inspector Southerby, that was his name," she announced. "When his officers had finished taking my statement, he came over and told me that, unfortunately, Andy hadn't made it and they were treating it as murder! Murder in our village, in our train station!"

"Oh, my goodness!" piped up Barbara. "It's really scary to think we have a killer on the loose in our village! I don't think I'll go out unless it's absolutely necessary."

"Now, you can't think like that, my dear," said June. "It's taken me long enough to get you out into the front of the shop. You can't start going backwards now!" Barbara jumped up and started tidying up to separate herself from further conversation.

"So, Pauline, what are your plans for the rest of the day?" asked Howard, offering another attempt to lighten the mood.

"Well, I'd better get back to the shop and open up, I suppose. Thank you for the tea and, before I go, could I just have a bag of sugar while I'm here? Mine hasn't turned up yet this week."

"Of course, Pauline," replied June, who swiftly called out, "Barbara, when you've put away the whisky and cups, can you fetch Pauline a bag of sugar, please?"

At that moment, everyone and everything seemed to return to the usual status quo. June stood up and unlocked the shop door, albeit a little wobbly initially, and Barbara returned to her usual nervous self, scurrying off to find a bag of sugar.

"I'll walk back with you, Pauline. I'd better take Charlie with me this time, though," Howard said as he turned to June and thanked her for looking after his dog. "Anytime you like, my dear. If there's a killer on the loose, I'd prefer to keep Charlie here all the time. Anyway, here's your sugar, Pauline."

Pauline paid and thanked June and Barbara for their kindness. "See you later then," said June who began straightening the sweets on the front counter.

Howard took Charlie by the lead, who was now keen to get going, and said, "Come on then Pauline, let's get you back to that shop of yours in one piece. You've had quite an eventful week so far, haven't you? I never did take you to A&E with that cut on your hand. Is it all right now?"

"Well, look," said Pauline, holding out her hand to show him. "I've still got a bandage on it, but that's more to keep any muck off. It can get quite muddy in the shop at times. I suppose, if I'm honest, I should've had some stitches, but I reckon I did quite a good DIY job myself. I found some butterfly stitches in my medicine box."

As they got closer, she looked up and saw several people standing outside her shop. "Oh, I hope they haven't been waiting out there for long."

"I reckon they have, Pauline. I think it's the same old gits I almost bumped into earlier." Pauline laughed and said, "You can't call them that, Howard!"

"And yet I did," he chuckled. "Anyway, I bet the village's jungle drums have been doing their job. I bet half of them have stuck around to find out why you're late and if you know anything. I don't think they've got anything else to do. Are you in the right frame of mind to open the shop? If you like, I can take Charlie home and come back and help you."

"No, don't worry. I'll be fine." She took a deep breath and walked up to them, saying confidently, "Good morning, ladies. Sorry to keep you waiting. If you can just give me five or ten minutes to get sorted, then I'll open up."

Howard tied Charlie outside and, turning to the crowd, said, "Don't worry, ladies. He doesn't bite. Just don't get him too excited!" He followed Pauline into the shop to double-check she was okay.

"You are a bugger with those women, Howard, teasing them like that!" As she headed towards the till, with the float, she flicked on the shop lights as she passed the universal switch. "Anyone would think you've been drinking," she added with a grin.

"What me? On a weekday morning? There's as much chance of me doing that as you, Pauline." They laughed as they realised that the brisk walk back had sent a rather large splash of whisky to their heads.

Howard checked his watch and, realising the day was disappearing quickly, said, "I'd best be going then but, if you need anything, you must ring me or Seraphina. I know you have our number, so don't be afraid to use it, please."

Pauline smiled warmly at him, feeling grateful for his thoughtfulness. "Go, be gone with you. I'll be fine now, but thanks. I really do appreciate your kindness."

As he came out of the shop, the women were fussing over Charlie. "What a lovely dog you have. He's got such a nice temperament," said one of them. This was quickly followed by another, asking, "Do you know why Pauline was late?" Another piped up, "Never mind about that, have you heard about the trouble at the train station? There's been a massacre; 'a terrorist attack' I heard someone say as they walked past us earlier!"

Howard smiled politely, realising the village's jungle drums were doing a great job, providing just enough information to let people jump to conclusions. He noted the idea to use in his book.

"Thanks very much for petting my dog. I expect he loved every minute." He untied Charlie and got away, without being drawn into any more conversation about the train station 'massacre' and started walking the last leg home.

As he strolled along, he couldn't help but wonder about the motive behind the stabbing. It didn't seem like a terrorist attack. As he walked, he noticed the beauty of the surrounding village; the soft chirping of birds; the gentle breeze rustling the leaves and the scent of fresh flowers from residents' hanging baskets. Such a far cry, he thought, from the recent tragedy, which had left a bitter taste in his mouth. However, as an aspiring author, he couldn't help but see the potential for a gripping story. As June had commented earlier, no one would have expected such an awful thing to occur in this quaint little village.

When he arrived home, he settled Charlie and made himself a cup of coffee before heading to his study. Strangely, he felt inspired to continue writing. However, before he could dive in, he needed to research the details of the next day's trip to Kew Gardens. He wanted everything to be ready when Seraphina returned later.

After a quick planning session, he had sorted their itinerary for the trip, from the opening times to which train to catch, and even where they could grab a bite to eat. He felt satisfied with the preparations and, with everything in order, could finally focus on his writing.

He had struggled with his story over the last few days, but now he was feeling inspired and keen to make everything fit neatly into his plot. Seeking inspiration, he regularly looked over his past diaries, believing that fact was often stranger than fiction. With years of entries chronicling office tiffs, affairs and twists, he had plenty of material to draw from, though he would obviously need to change the occasional name.

As he perused his diaries, he realised that none of them had included murder, and he was seriously considering adding one to his current plot. He set his alarm for 4 pm, knowing from experience that, once he started mulling over the idea and writing, time would fly by. He didn't want a repeat of the previous evening. Tonight, he wanted to have everything under control, and after deciding against his earlier suggestion of a takeaway, he would have a delicious homemade meal ready, ensuring a great start to the weekend.

He was fully immersed in his creative flow, thoroughly enjoying himself as he crafted his story. His main character was about to get caught in the photocopier room with a colleague from another department, revealing insider dealing, when the alarm clock interrupted his writing. 'Damn,' he thought, but quickly realised that it was best to step away while he still had a clear idea of what would happen next. He closed his computer and headed to the kitchen to prepared dinner.

EIGHT

Friday evening

Seraphina had just finished a productive day in the office and Chris jingled his keys as he came down the stairs. He looked ready to leave. He walked over to her desk and asked, "Seraphina, would it be okay if you close the office today? I almost forgot about some dry cleaning I need for tomorrow, and I should make it there before it closes if I leave now."

Seraphina smiled and replied, "Yes, of course, that's fine. You're the boss, after all! I'm flattered that you trust me."

"It's funny, isn't it? You can work with someone for years and hardly know them. Take Margaret, my last assistant. We worked together for years, but the office always felt very formal. I feel like I've known you for years already. You've brought the energy back into the office." He paused and smiled, reflecting on their working relationship. "You make me happy to be here," he added.

Seraphina felt a little embarrassed and surprised to feel her cheeks warm. "Oh, are you referring to the goings-on at the pub last night? I'm so sorry about that."

"Ah, forget about it," Chris laughed. "People always react differently when a new person moves into the village. Some are welcoming, while others take their time to decide whether to befriend them or not. Then some are just miserable gits. Think of last night as an initiation ceremony."

He smiled and continued, "Everyone who needs to know, now knows who you and Howard are. They can either like it or lump it but, in my book, you're in." Glancing at the clock, he exclaimed, "Oh, hell! I'll have to rush if I'm going to make it before closing. Have a fabulous weekend. Maybe I'll see you in the pub if you're out. I will be there at some point."

She wished him a lovely weekend and, as he rushed out of the door, the little bell above it rattled like mad.

Seraphina checked the clock. It was 4:50 pm. Chris would have to hurry, she thought, or he wouldn't make it. Should she call the dry cleaners and let them know he was on his way? Maybe they stay open until 5:30 pm. As she closed the computer programs and locked away her paperwork, she pondered. Chris was a grown man and could handle his own affairs, she decided. She was an accountant, not his personal assistant, even if she felt an unexplainable urge to look after him. She stood up and was about to grab her jacket when the doorbell rang and Ziggy walked in. He was back in his scruffy clothes. Seraphina was slightly surprised but quietly pleased, as she greeted him, "Oh, hello there. How are you?"

"All the better for seeing you, my dear," he said. "Have you recovered from last night?

"Ah, yes, we seemed to be the main attraction last night. I told Chris earlier how embarrassing it all was. Thanks for manhandling that Mike person."

"No worries. If there's one thing I'm good at, it's manhandling," he said, winking at Seraphina as he flexed his biceps in front of her. She didn't know where to look, as she felt her cheeks warm.

"Was there something you needed, Ziggy?"

"Where's Chris? I was wondering if he's up for early doors. Is he not here?"

"No, he left just a few minutes ago. He said he needed to catch the dry cleaners before they closed."

"Well, that's a shame. I suppose I can't tempt you to a quickie on your way home?" he grinned, as he teased her.

As he expected, she declined. "No thanks, Ziggy. I don't want to bump into that nasty man again. But ten out of ten for trying," she said, smiling.

"God loves a trier," Ziggy said, giving a huge belly laugh. "Right, I'm off to the pub then. You have a lovely weekend, and I hope to see you soon." He reached up and made the little doorbell ring, just as he had done last time.

Seraphina was not sure if Ziggy was just being friendly or flirting with her. Was he naturally a flirt? Some men are, she thought. She couldn't work him out. Whatever he said, no matter how cheekily, there was always an element of charm. She was annoyed with herself for blushing around him. For all his scruffy appearance, she had to admit that there was something undeniably attractive about him.

She set the burglar alarm and headed for the door. She gave the handle a gentle push and pull to double-check that the office door was locked properly before she headed home. As she walked, she thought about Ziggy and how she had been pleasantly surprised by his intelligence during the previous night's quiz. His strength had also proven to be an asset, as he fearlessly stepped in to help them.

She turned the corner where her house came into view, which forced her to focus on the upcoming weekend with

Howard. She eagerly wondered what he had planned for their trip the following day and pushed any distracting thoughts of Ziggy aside.

"Hi, I'm home," she called out, as she walked through the front door. The rattle of a saucepan lid reached her ears as she took off her coat and hung it up. A quick sniff of the air revealed that Howard had prepared spaghetti bolognese for dinner. She couldn't help but think how he had become a proficient cook over the past few months, although she quickly reminded herself that he had ample time to practise since he was currently unemployed. Silently scolding herself for entertaining such negative thoughts, she resolved to enjoy the weekend with him.

Though she never admitted it, she was grateful to have her meal ready and the house nice and tidy when she returned home every evening. "Hi, how are you? Something smells delicious!" she said, kicking off her shoes, sliding into her slippers and heading towards the Aga.

Howard turned around and greeted her with a smile. "Hi, Sweetheart, have you got the wine?"

"No. Was I supposed to?"

"I sent you a text asking if you could collect a bottle or two from the off-licence on your way home."

"I never got a text, but you know what the signal's like round here, it's so temperamental. Do you want me to pop out now?" Just then Seraphina's phone pinged and the text arrived. "Oh there it is now, whoops!"

"Don't worry, dinner still needs a few more minutes, so I'll nip out myself. I'll turn the heat down, but can you just stir the spaghetti a couple of times to make sure it doesn't stick? I'll be back in a jiffy."

He hastily grabbed his jacket and dashed out of the house, determined to make the evening perfect. He soon arrived at the shop and was surprised to see a small queue had formed. Glancing down the line, he spotted Sarah at the counter, struggling with her crutches. She was the last person he wanted to see. As she approached him, a magazine she had rolled up under her arm slipped and fell to the floor. He felt compelled to help and swiftly picked it up, offering it to her with a polite smile. "Hi Sarah, fancy seeing you here. There you go, do have a nice evening won't you."

Sarah thanked him for the magazine, smiled and carried on without stopping. She seemed to have her mind elsewhere that evening, much to Howard's relief. He was soon served and made it back home just in time to save the dinner from spoiling.

"Hi, Sweetheart, I'm back," he called as he dashed through the kitchen and over to the stove.

"Here, can you put one of these on the table and the other in the fridge. Then, if you take a seat, dinner will be ready in just a minute. Flinging his jacket over the kitchen sofa and smiling at her he continued, "Why don't you help yourself to a glass of wine, now we have some?"

"Well, thank you very much, kind sir," she quipped as she reach for the bottle opener, smiling. "This is the life."

Dinner was soon on the table, and they both tucked into spaghetti bolognese and garlic bread. "Tell me about your day then, Darling," Howard enquired.

"It was nice and quiet. Just what I wanted, especially after last night, and I got a lot done." Twisting the spaghetti around her fork, she took a mouthful of the delicious meal and was about to continue when Howard interjected.

"Don't speak with your mouth full, Dear! You always tell me off for that," he said with a chuckle.

"There was one interesting surprise though. What kind of work do you think Ziggy does? Come on, take a guess!" she urged with enthusiasm.

"I have no idea, do I?" he responded, with a hint of irritation that she had mentioned Ziggy's name again. He tried anyway as he didn't want to start the weekend off on the wrong note. "Now then, you said he looked like a tramp when he initially called in the office, but he didn't when I saw him at the pub. Maybe those were his work clothes. Is he a builder? After all, he seemed quite fit." He waited for her response.

"No," she replied. "Try again."

"Give me a clue then."

"Okay, well, he does use paint and builds things, but not what you would expect. Have another guess. I only found out today when I got started on his 'shoe box' of an accounting system!" she explained with some excitement.

"Flippin' heck, Seraphina. It could be anything. Hmm, let me eat my dinner and have a think. How's yours?"

"It's lovely. It tastes a little different though now that you ask. I like it more. What have you done to it?"

"I used my new recipe book. The one your mother bought me for Christmas. Turns out it's a good book." She smiled and said, "Well, I'm glad she got you a useful present, at last." He grinned. "I think I'll try out some more recipes. Maybe I'll surprise you with something new next weekend."

"I'll look forward to it," she replied, as Ziggy and his job faded from her thoughts. "Speaking of next weekend, what have you planned for this one?"

"Okay, so I've done some research. I started with the train timetable. Oh, wait a minute." He sat up straight, raised his voice, and announced, "Oh, my god, I can't believe that I almost forgot about this. There's been a murder at the train station!"

"No, you're joking!" Seraphina exclaimed, her eyes wide with surprise. "Who was it? Do we know them? When did it happen, and how? And in little old Smallsville, as well!"

Her curiosity was piqued, and more than a hint of excitement coursed through her veins. Despite the tragic news, she suddenly felt alive, but for all the wrong reasons. She couldn't believe such a crime had occurred in their small community.

"Please, hold nothing back," she urged. "You must tell me everything."

"Well," Howard began, "after I left you at work, I walked Charlie and ended up getting to the corner shop later than usual. I waited for ages for my latte, because…"

Seraphina cut in, her tone impatient. "Please, cut to the chase. Who was it and how did it happen? I didn't ask for a blow-by-blow account of your day. Just the action, please."

"Okay, okay," he said, with more than a hint of irritation creeping into his voice. "A man was stabbed on the platform and died. Nobody knows who did it. That's the gist of it. Happy now?" His frustration was palpable, and he couldn't help feeling annoyed by her impatience.

Sensing his annoyance, Seraphina quickly gave a half-hearted effort of an apology. "I'm sorry, but there's no need to get stroppy." She took the last mouthful of spaghetti and mumbled through her food, "This is a lovely meal," while trying to smile at the same time.

She could be cuttingly sarcastic at times but, even with her mouth full and her smile wonky, Howard couldn't help but notice how her face lit up and how beautiful she looked when she smiled. "You know, you have the most amazing smile," he said, pouring her another glass of wine. "That's one of the many reasons I fell in love with you."

"Stop it, you great softy," she said, taking a sip of her wine.

Howard grinned, feeling pleased with himself. "All right, all right. Let me start again. So, I went to the corner shop, got a paper, and sat outside with Charlie. Then a group of people rushed by, looking flustered, and some of them called in the shop. I thought June had forgotten my order as I'd waited so long, so I went back in to remind her. That's when she told me what had happened although, at that point, we only thought someone had been stabbed. Even so, it was a shock, and the news had visibly shaken June. She closed the shop temporarily and kindly invited me to stay. She's a bit of a sly one, though. She was ever so quick to ask Barbara to grab a bottle of whisky and put a dash in all our coffee cups."

Seraphina chuckled. "You know, Howard, I've heard she's a bit of a cougar. You want to be careful spending time with older ladies!"

"Well, Barbara was there too."

"Two older ladies! You devil!" she teased, smiling broadly.

"Anyway, after that, I came home; only to realise that I'd left Charlie at the shop. When I returned to pick him up; by the way, June loves Charlie and said if ever we need a sitter, she would gladly have him. Anyway, I digress. I'd only been there a minute when Pauline came in. You know, Pauline, that runs the grocers."

Seraphina nodded in acknowledgement as she took a large gulp of wine from her glass and gestured for him to continue.

"Pauline was a little shaky. Anyway, it turned out the guy almost died in her arms. She'd come straight from the train station after giving her statement. June, being June, promptly closed the shop again, sat us down, and made us all sweet tea topped up with whisky. Actually, she got Barbara to make it again!" He paused for breath and looked at Seraphina, who was now perched on the edge of her chair, waiting for him to continue.

"Well, June skilfully and politely got a full statement of events from Pauline. I wouldn't be surprised if she'd got a better account of events from her than the police did."

He continued to tell her all the finer details, and Seraphina couldn't believe her ears. Taking another sip of wine, she asked, "I wonder who did it and why? I know this is going to sound bad, but I hope there was a specific reason and not just some looney going around, stabbing people!"

"I guess only time will tell, but it's not the sort of thing I would have expected here. It's normally so peaceful."

"Speak for yourself. What about all those boy racers we hear? I bet there's more going on in this small village than we ever imagined." Seraphina was intrigued, as she headed to the large comfy sofa in the kitchen corner.

Howard tidied away the dinner plates as she kicked off her shoes, grabbed her phone and began ploughing through her emails.

NINE

Friday evening – after dinner

"It's such a nice evening. Why don't we sit out on the patio? We could brainstorm ideas for the garden," suggested Howard.

"Yes, why not? I'm really looking forward to Kew Gardens. I've wanted to go for years," replied Seraphina.

It was a lovely evening as they strolled around the garden, discussing various ideas, such as adding a patio here or there, building a fishpond, and installing a pergola or firepit. The ideas kept flowing as they explored every corner of the garden.

Finally, they returned to the patio and settled into their ageing garden chairs. They sat in silence, enjoying the peace, as their minds turned to the events of the previous night. They could no longer avoid the inevitable conversation and they began to speak at the same time.

"Look," began Seraphina, "I want to talk about last night."

"I was just about to bring that up."

After a brief exchange of 'you first, no, you first,' Seraphina took the lead.

"I wanted to explain about the other evening and how I ended up in the pub. Chris signed up two new customers and he was feeling pleased with himself. I was pleased for him as well, so, when he suggested closing a little early to celebrate at the local pub, I thought, Damn it, yes. Why not? It felt a little like old times, you know - work hard, play hard - like we used to."

As she finished speaking, she looked to the ground and sadness showed on her face. Howard could only sit and listen, as he could see that she was not happy.

"There's nothing going on between Chris and me," she continued. "He's my boss, and that's all there is to it. When I got home after the pub, where, I would like to add, I only had two drinks, you had prepared a lovely meal and I felt bad about being late. You kept topping up my glass and, before I knew it, I'd finished the entire bottle. I had to go straight to bed as I felt so drunk that I practically passed out as soon as I hit the pillow. I'm sorry. I guess it just took more effect than usual. As for that chap down the pub having a go at me, I have no idea where that came from."

She paused for a couple of seconds before saying, "Howard, I've been wondering lately if moving here was the right thing to do."

Howard took her hand. "I'm sorry I've made you feel that way. I guess I've been feeling a little lost lately as well. It's nice to pass the time of day with the locals, but it's not a patch on the hustle and bustle of city life, is it? I suppose it'll take us both some getting used to."

He paused, expecting her to say something. She remained silent, so he continued. "That chap Spencer, the one that had a go at you in the pub. I understand he's just not a very cheerful guy. I've been told he has a bit of a downer on women for some unknown reason. Earlier that day, when I walked Charlie, in my haste to get to the butchers, I walked across the cricket green. I suppose I didn't really think about where I was going, but Spencer saw me. He'd been out checking the green for the game. I heard someone shouting from a distance but didn't think he meant me. That's why he started on me in the pub."

"I see," said Seraphina. "But what was all that stuff about with that guy they called Mike? You know, the one that Ziggy dragged out of the pub?"

Howard hesitated, unsure of how to explain the situation. He offered to top up Seraphina's glass before he finally began. "Well, I was in the shop the other morning, as I always am, and this woman came in, stumbling on crutches. She asked for a coffee and said how she hoped she wouldn't miss her train. Well, somehow, I ended up offering to carry her bag and coffee as she hobbled down Station Street to catch her train."

Seraphina raised her eyebrows, listening intently. "It would appear that this woman is Mike's wife. So, I guess he must have found out and wasn't very pleased about it. It was a bit of an overreaction if you ask me, but there you go."

"I see. Does this woman have a name then?"

"Her name is Sarah. I don't know what she does for a living. Just that she works in the city, and she broke her ankle a few weeks ago." He tried to lighten the conversation by deliberately steering it away from Mike.

As Seraphina sipped her drink, she pondered over the revelations. She felt a mix of emotions. Was she annoyed? Jealous, perhaps? Strangely enough, she suddenly felt a pang of guilt. She realised she had been so preoccupied with her job and, more recently, thoughts of Ziggy that she had neglected Howard lately. She had to admit to herself that all she had focused on was when he would get a job.

She took a deep breath and calmed down. She reminded herself how she trusted Howard and that their relationship was built on a strong foundation of mutual respect and love. What if he was just helping someone to the train station out of kindness and the woman, sadly, had a jealous husband? It really wasn't a big deal.

Howard wasn't sure how she was going to react, so he patiently waited for a reply. Eventually, after what seemed like an age, he asked, "Are you still with me? You seem to have drifted off into your own world there."

He hadn't told the whole truth, as he had omitted the part about helping Sarah twice. He had almost convinced himself he had done nothing wrong, and that it was his imagination making him feel guilty. Seraphina's silence was making him feel slightly uncomfortable, as she sat gazing at the garden.

Eventually, she replied, "You know what? You're right. This village seems like a tight-knit community where everyone knows each other's business. If someone got up to no good, they wouldn't get away with it for long, because someone else would shout about it, probably in the pub. When I think about it, I guess we were the centre of attention for a while last night. But I've decided that I won't let this bother me. What about you?"

Howard felt a huge sense of relief at her reaction and smiled, saying, "Exactly. And no, I'm not going to let this bother me either. We've got better things to think of than a jealous husband."

Seraphina replied in a gentle voice, "We need time to adjust to our new life, Howard. You don't have to find a job urgently, I know, but spending all day alone is not good for you either. What do you usually do apart from having coffee with those ladies at the corner shop? And have you thought about what you'd like to do? What jobs have you considered?"

She was on a roll with her job questions again and it made him hesitate. He was still unsure if he should share his recent venture of writing a novel, but her blunt questions made him realise that he couldn't keep it to himself forever. He knew she would be supportive but, as he planned to finish the book within the following week, he decided he would wait and tell her then.

"Well, are you going to tell me or not?" she asked, as her emotions swung backwards and forwards. She desperately wanted to be the understanding wife, but just couldn't stop herself sometimes.

"I thought we should work on the garden before I started another job. Remember how helpful it was when I was around during the house renovations?"

"I see. Well, please keep your eye out, won't you? You know the right job always comes along when you're not looking."

Howard defended himself by replying, "You're probably right. I've already uploaded my CV to all the job sites and I've spoken to several agencies. But it's hard, you know. They all want to offer me a job doing what I've just left. It's extremely discouraging. Changing one's career direction turns out to be more of a challenge than I ever expected."

He looked down at his drink, and Seraphina watched him closely. It suddenly dawned on her how difficult the situation must be for him and she felt guilty for putting him under so much pressure.

"I'm really sorry. I've never thought of it like that. Since I've known you, you've always been a business success. I'm sure the right thing will come along, just at the right time. It always does. Just look at my job," she added, trying to offer some encouragement.

"Thanks. It's good to know you can see it from my point of view, eventually."

Ziggy and his occupation popped back into Seraphina's head and, as she was now keen to change the subject, she exclaimed, "Oh my god, you never finished guessing what Ziggy's occupation is! Go on. Have another guess, please." She was bursting to tell him.

"Okay, okay, it seems you're not willing to let this one drop. Well, let me see. You said something about paint and scruffy clothes, but he's not a builder. Maybe he's a painter and decorator? That's the paint covered, and a grave digger in his spare time. That would be why he was wearing the wellies!" he teased.

"What! You're not even giving this a good guess, are you? I'll tell you then. He's an artist and a sculptor."

Howard was silent. Seraphina, who was expecting a response, even a sarcastic one, continued with her enthusiastic chatter. "I bet he was working on a sculpture in someone's large garden or maybe a public place. That's why he was so dirty! Or perhaps he was delivering one? Did you hear about the big sculpture that was installed in the neighbouring town recently? Maybe it was one of his creations! Initially, I didn't peg him as the creative type, but now it all makes perfect sense."

Without giving Howard a chance to speak, she continued, "I thought the names on his invoices were referring to buildings he worked at, not the names of his pieces. Based on what I've seen so far, he seems to be quite successful. Oh, my goodness, Howard! What if he's a famous sculptor, and we didn't even know it?"

As she spoke, her excitement grew and her mind raced with the possibilities. Howard waited patiently for her to catch her breath, then finally broke his silence, by saying, "I never would have guessed that in a million years. But to be fair, he is a little flamboyant, isn't he? What sort of income are you talking about then?"

"You know I can't discuss that. GDPR, and all that. But, you know, the price of his last invoice was the same as your end-of-year bonus last year! And we were both pleased with that, weren't we?"

Her mind was reeling. Ziggy was handsome, single, and rich and, as far as she could see, he had been making eyes at her from the minute they met. She would have to play it cool.

Howard interrupted her thoughts. "Come on then, let's google him. Most artists have some publicity. If he's that good, it should be easy to find him. I'll fire up the desktop in the office, we never get a decent signal out here on my mobile."

He headed off to the study while Seraphina picked up their drinks and followed him. After waxing lyrically about Ziggy, she felt she may have got a little carried away and didn't want to appear overly keen or interested.

Looking up at the clock in the study, she exclaimed, "Blimey, look. It's 9:30 pm already. At this rate, we'll never get up in time for the train tomorrow. Let's do this another time. It's not that important and your desktop takes an age to get started."

She was too late as Howard insisted. "Come on. It won't take long. We'll have a quick look and then call it a night. Look. It's almost ready. There we go. Now what did you call him? Ziggy Palmer? Surely that can't be his real name. Nothing's going to come up with that name, is it?"

He tapped it into the keyboard as he was speaking. "Well, would you look at that! Your Mr Palmer is at the top of the search engine, with images and everything. Looks like he might be someone, after all."

"He's not my 'Mr Palmer', thank you," she snapped back. Just then, it occurred to Howard that she might have a soft spot for Ziggy. They got on well the other night, and she had mentioned him a few times since meeting him. Howard raised his eyebrows in surprise at her defensive response but decided not to tease her any further. He calmly replied, "I didn't mean it like that. I just meant he was your customer."

She took a deep breath, realising she had overreacted. "I'm sorry, Howard. I didn't mean to snap at you. Tell me what it says, please. I can't see a thing without my glasses."

"Ziggy Palmer, only son of the wealthy self-made business tycoon, David Palmer. Date of birth ..."

She interrupted, by saying, "No, not the family stuff, his arty stuff."

"Wait a minute, don't you think it's interesting about his father? Obviously not then. Let me just scan through and pick out the best parts."

As he scanned the document, he called out the title of some pieces of art. "There's 'Mermaids' which is in that large shopping centre in Throxton, and 'Horsefire' at Theakston Hall. I think I've seen that one! Wasn't that the one that was lit up with red and orange lights at Christmas, with water flowing over it? I'm sure I saw it on TV. Very nice, actually." He continued to read out the titles of the other pieces.

"I'm off to get my glasses. I think they're in the kitchen. I'll be right back," said Seraphina.

Howard reached the end of the article and continued searching to see what else he could find. The next heading wasn't so complimentary. 'Local artist in expensive split.'

He read on and discovered that Ziggy had been married about twenty years ago. It seemed that his wife left him, convinced he was having an affair with an unnamed person. Howard flicked to the next article, which was about the unveiling of another sculpture. In all the pictures, Ziggy had a constant companion by his side; his friend Chris. A realisation dawned on him. They had said how they had been through a lot together. Maybe they were more than friends; maybe they were partners, and Seraphina hadn't realised.

Howard could hear her coming back down the hall. He whizzed back to the first article. Should he tell her? What if he was wrong? And even if she had a soft spot for Ziggy, she wouldn't do anything about it, would she? His mind raced as he wondered if she was harbouring thoughts about Ziggy like he was about the beautiful Sarah. He scolded himself. This was ridiculous, he thought, as she walked in. "Okay, let me see. How famous is he?" asked Seraphina.

Howard stood up. He decided to let destiny take its course and gestured towards the chair. "Here, take a seat. You'll be able to see everything better that way."

She read the article and was thrilled to discover she was on first-name terms with a famous artist. "Look, he's exhibited all over the place, even at the Tate Gallery. You've got to be someone to be there, and we had no idea!" She beamed as she turned to look at Howard.

She was alive again, and he didn't want to burst her bubble.

"Well, would you believe it? We were on the same quiz team, and he never said a word! But I guess he's not likely to introduce himself saying, 'Hi, I'm a famous artist,' is he?"

With excitement in her voice, she announced, "Wait till I tell Beth. I haven't spoken to her for ages, and we're due for a catch-up. Now I'll have something really interesting to say."

She was thrilled to find out that Ziggy was 'someone' and would revel in telling everyone she knew, especially her ex-colleagues.

TEN

Friday late evening

Remembering their plans for Kew Gardens, Howard said, "Now, let's talk about tomorrow. I thought we would catch the early train. That way, we can get there at a decent time and maybe have some breakfast or, if you like, we can go first class and have breakfast on the train. Have you seen the size of the place?"

Seraphina smiled in agreement and replied, "Yes, there's definitely lots to see. Let's go first class, if we can." She was excited at the prospect of exploring the gardens.

Howard nodded and said, "Apparently, it's the largest botanical garden in the world, with over 50,000 different plant species. It should be quite the day out." He rubbed his hands together in anticipation.

"I'm excited for the day already. I can't wait to explore it all!" exclaimed Seraphina.

"Absolutely! It will be a perfect day out. I'm looking forward to it too. It'll be great to get away, even for one day," replied Howard.

"Yes, it will. Can you just flick to Kew's website so we can have a little look now please?"

Howard was delighted with how the evening was going and, after calling up the website for Kew Gardens, he passed Seraphina the mouse so she could explore. Sitting back into his chair he savoured the anticipation of their upcoming adventure as his worries and doubts began to fade.

Suddenly, the tranquillity of the evening was shattered by the sound of breaking glass, followed by a loud thud. Charlie barked madly, and Seraphina jumped out of her seat.

"What the hell?" Howard exclaimed, and his mind immediately raced through all possible scenarios. Had something fallen? Was someone breaking in?

They rushed to where they thought the sound had come from. When they reached the entrance hall, they saw broken glass on the floor. In the middle of the hall, they found a brick with a piece of paper attached to it with a red rubber band.

"Don't touch it," shouted Seraphina urgently. "I've seen this sort of thing on TV, and you shouldn't add your fingerprints and mess up the evidence."

"Bloody hell, Seraphina, this isn't a TV program! This is real life!" Howard exclaimed in a stern voice. "I'll call the police. Don't forget that someone was killed in the village this morning!"

He fumbled around in his pocket, searching for his mobile, muttering under his breath, "I don't even know the number of the local police station. I wish I had one of those business cards the police gave to Pauline."

Meanwhile, Seraphina made her way over to the landline phone in the kitchen and dialled 111 with a sense of calm determination. Howard followed slowly and, as he continued to search for a phone number, he heard her say,

"Hello, we need the police. There's been a strange incident at our house."

After a brief exchange, she hung up the phone and turned to him.

"All sorted. The police are on their way," she informed him in an unusually calm voice. "They shouldn't be long now. So, what do you think is on the paper?"

"I haven't got a clue but look what they've done to our window." His anger rose at the sight of the shattered diamond-leaded window. "That's going to cost a pretty penny to fix. It's an original window. Who knows how old it is? We can forget about going out tomorrow with this mess to deal with."

He knelt to examine the mark the brick had made on the floor and tried to console himself by saying, "I guess we're lucky we have these big flagstones; it might have cracked lesser tiles."

He looked up and saw that Seraphina had lost her composure and was now crying. He rushed over to her side and tried to comfort her by putting his arms around her, but she pushed him away. "I've struggled to settle here and now look. God knows what the message in there says!" she sobbed.

Howard felt a pang of worry as he saw how much the broken window and ominous note had affected her. "We'll get through this, don't worry. It's just a broken window and a note. We don't even know what it says yet," he said, trying to console her.

Meanwhile, just a few streets away, Inspector Southerby and his assistant, Detective Constable Hicks, were wrapping up another call when Hicks's radio beeped with an incoming message. "Yes, we're not far," she replied.

"We'll head there next." She clipped her radio back onto her jacket and ushered the inspector towards the door.

"What have we got then, Hicks? I was hoping to call it a night," said the inspector.

"Looks like we have a household disturbance but, as uniform will take over an hour to get there and we're just around the corner, I agreed we'd take the call. It shouldn't take long. I hope you don't mind?"

The inspector took off his reading glasses and placed them carefully in his top pocket, as he spoke. "Well, it's a bit late now if I did. Lucky for you, I don't." Smiling, he continued, "Right. What do you know about this disturbance, and where are we going?"

"We can walk from here as it's only around the corner. I'll tell you all about it on the way." They said their goodbyes to the existing call and left.

Hicks explained to Inspector Southerby as they walked briskly towards the scene of the crime, "The caller reported a brick through a window with some kind of note attached to it. Doesn't sound very nice, does it?"

As they turned the corner and walked up to the cottage, they could see the broken window. When they arrived, they peered through the window and saw the shattered glass strewn across the floor inside. Hicks reached for her camera. "Shall I take some pictures before we knock?" she asked the inspector.

"Yes, good idea," he replied. "Let's document the scene before we disturb anything."

Hicks snapped a few quick shots from the outside and the inspector scanned the street, looking for potential witnesses. He turned to Hicks and asked, "Have you got that list of out-of-hours traders? Whoever lives here will need it, I'm sure."

The inspector studied the broken window. It was clear that it was not a random act of vandalism. Someone had deliberately targeted the house.

"Ready as ever, Sir. It's all on my phone," Hicks replied as she scrolled through the list. "We've got a locksmith, a glazier, and a few other emergency repair services."

"Good work, Hicks," the inspector said, nodding in approval. "Right then, if you're ready, 'let's just do this', as you youngsters say."

"No, Sir, it's either 'just do it' or 'let's do this'. You've mixed them up again. You are funny."

"You're not laughing at me again, are you Hicks?"

"Oh no, Sir, never, Sir," she replied quickly, still smiling.

"What are you waiting for? Go ahead and ring the doorbell. Let's see if we can find any clues inside."

Howard's heart leapt into his throat when the doorbell rang. "That can't possibly be the police already," he muttered, as he glanced at his watch. "You only rang them five minutes ago."

Seraphina looked at him, with concern etched over her face. "What should we do?"

"Just to be safe, you wait here in the kitchen," he said, with a firm yet reassuring tone. "We don't know who it is yet. I'll answer the door."

As Howard passed the coat cupboard, he paused and opened the cupboard door. He quickly scanned for something he could use to defend himself if needed. His eyes fell on a spare golf club he kept there for just this kind of situation. Living in London for so many years had taught him to be prepared for anything. He reached for the club and felt a sense of reassurance as he gripped its familiar handle.

The front door was solid wood, which made it impossible to see who was on the other side. Howard peered through the new hole in the window and saw a middle-aged man in a suit and a younger woman next to him, also smartly dressed. He didn't recognise either of them. He decided that it was better to be safe than sorry and called out from the window, "Hello, can I help you?"

The inspector moved over to the damaged window. "Good evening, Sir," he said, as he flashed his badge. "I'm Inspector Southerby and this is Detective Constable Hicks. I understand you reported a disturbance. I hope you don't mind, but we've already had a look around outside and taken a few photographs from this side of the window. My DC has the number for an emergency glazier for you. Do you think we could step inside? I assume you're Mr Buchanan. Is that right?"

"Ah, yes, forgive me. I'll just get the door." Howard quickly returned the golf club to the cupboard and opened the heavy front door. Seraphina, who had been watching from the kitchen doorway, stepped forward into the hall. The inspector and his DC entered briskly, and Hicks gently closed the door behind them.

"You were prompt. I'm surprised you didn't see who did it," said Howard, as he gestured them deeper into the house.

"We were on a call just around the corner, Mr Buchanan," replied Inspector Southerby, "but we'll do our best to catch the culprit. Now, can you tell me what happened here?" He smiled and looked at Seraphina.

"Inspector, this is my wife, Seraphina."

"Nice to meet you, Mrs Buchanan. Does anyone else live here with you and your husband?"

"No, it's just the two of us."

Howard quickly recounted the events of their evening and explained how they found the brick and saw the note. The inspector listened carefully, and Hicks recorded the details in her notebook as they spoke.

"We haven't looked at the note yet though. My wife said we shouldn't touch it. She's quite the sleuth sometimes, you know." He put his arm around her shoulder again and hoped she wouldn't push him away this time, as he continued, "She said it would be wrong to contaminate it with our fingerprints, didn't you, Darling? I told her she watches way too many TV mysteries."

The inspector moved towards Seraphina. "Mrs Buchanan, Seraphina, what a pretty name that is. Now then, you were absolutely right not to touch the evidence. Shall we see what this note on the brick says? Hicks, can you get it for me?"

Without delay, Hicks took further pictures of the crime scene from indoors before disturbing it. Then she put on a pair of stretchy plastic gloves, picked up the brick and put down a place marker in case they needed to study it further. She carefully took off the red rubber band and put it in a clear plastic specimen bag and sealed it. Slowly, she unwrapped the paper and held out the note so that the inspector could read it.

He seemed to spend an age looking at it, considering the content before he spoke. Seraphina and Howard both stood in silence, waiting. Eventually, the inspector read out loud, 'You're not welcome here. Leave now or suffer the consequences.'

DC Hicks then placed the brick and the note into separate specimen bags and the inspector reminded her to send everything straight to the lab. He then turned to Seraphina and Howard and asked, "Have either of you got any enemies or particularly upset someone lately?"

They exchanged a glance and Seraphina took a deep breath. Once she started talking, her words flowed rapidly and she became increasingly animated.

"I knew we shouldn't have moved. I never wanted to move. You know, Inspector, I've tried to make the best of it. We've only been here a few months, and to the local pub twice, maybe three times, but that's where all the trouble stems from, if you ask me. First, a strange man shouted at Howard about his precious cricket green. Then he had a go at me telling me how I couldn't stay out of the pub! Then another chap came in, shouting, and manhandled Howard, warning him to stay away from his wife! What is it with the people in this bloody place? They're all so paranoid about newcomers."

"Now come on Seraphina, it's not that bad. We've made friends here too, haven't we?" Howard said, as he tried to put his arm around her again, but she was having none of it this time. She was undeniably upset about the whole incident.

"I think a nice sweet cup of tea might be in order," the inspector suggested. "Hicks, do you have all the pictures you need of the crime scene?"

"Yes, Sir. All done."

Continuing to address Hicks, the inspector asked, "Can you help Mrs Buchanan … or do you prefer to be called Seraphina?" as he turned to Seraphina, who nodded. "Great. Hicks, can you please help Seraphina in the kitchen, while we tidy this mess up. I'll have a chat with Mr Buchanan."

DC Hicks quickly scanned the hallway for the direction of the kitchen, saying in a gentle voice, "Come on then, Seraphina. Let's leave them to it." They headed towards the kitchen, where Hicks spotted the kettle. "You sit yourself down. I'll make the tea."

Hicks had a friendly personality with a kind and pretty face. At first, Seraphina assumed she was only a few years younger than herself. However, as she watched her make the tea, she realised that her assessment was wrong. She appeared to be in her late 20s, or early 30s, with stunning plaited long blonde hair. Seraphina suddenly felt old, exposed, vulnerable, and helpless. Not only did she have a husband who appeared to be avoiding work, but someone had threatened them with a brick through their window. These last few days had been difficult for her.

"Do you have any idea why this has happened?" Hicks asked, as she passed Seraphina a sweet cup of tea.

That was all she needed to unleash the pent-up anger she'd had for some time. She told Hicks how they had come to live in the village, and how everything had kicked off when they went to the pub. She also complained that Howard didn't seem to be showing any intention of working. Eventually, she got around to talking about the smashed window.

"I'm sorry if I come across as a little harsh, but this is the final straw. My patience swings from being understanding to being furious. Sometimes I feel I'm going mad and now I think I've reached my wits' end."

Hicks listened carefully and made all the right noises in all the right places. She wrote nothing down, as she was confident that she would remember everything clearly to document later.

Seraphina liked her and enjoyed the much-missed female company. They talked about anything and everything for some considerable time.

"I know I shouldn't say this, especially as you're the police and here on business, but I'm really enjoying this chat. Even if it is for all the wrong reasons. Would you like another cup of tea? I've got some nice biscuits in the cupboard somewhere."

"Tea and biscuits I can accept all day long, thank you. I'm glad you feel a little better about things now. Tell me about your plans for the garden."

Meanwhile, Inspector Southerby had been interviewing Howard. "I think we can clear this away now. We have all the pictures we need. Do you have a dustpan and brush, Mr Buchanan? I wouldn't want that lovely dog of yours cutting his paws."

Howard turned to the cloakroom and opened the wooden latched door. He reached in and grabbed the broom. He passed it to the inspector and asked, "Can you hold on to this whilst I find the dustpan and brush?"

The inspector started to sweep up. Finding the dustpan and brush, Howard told the inspector, "Make a pile just here and I'll get it."

It was a perfect scene of domestic teamwork. As the inspector handed back the broom, he looked at the floor and smiled at their handiwork. "There, all done. Now, what shall we do about securing your window? Do you want this number I have for the 24-hour glaziers?"

"No thanks. I've got some plywood and duct tape in the shed. I'll use them to patch up the window on both sides and take care of it in the morning. If anyone tries to break in, I'm sure Charlie will bark. The window is quite old, so it will probably require a specialist to repair it. I hope you catch whoever did this."

"So do I, Mr Buchanan, so do I. Do you have any suspicions regarding the identity of the person who so kindly delivered the note by hand?"

"Shall we go to my office instead of standing here in the hallway? It's this way," Howard suggested, gesturing towards the study. He led the inspector down the corridor to his office at the end of the house. He hoped they would be far enough away from Seraphina so that she would not overhear their conversation.

"Please, Inspector, take a seat and let me tell you about my week. I can't help but feel I may have inadvertently played a role in what has happened, but my wife doesn't know the full truth. Although, I assure you, I have done nothing wrong. I believe I may have ruffled the feathers of a very jealous husband, which I fear might have led to some trouble."

Howard ran the inspector through his last few days, going over every detail. He described his daily routine, every interaction he had with people, and the events that led him to believe he may have angered someone. The inspector listened attentively, occasionally interrupting to ask questions and clarify details. Howard couldn't help but feel a sense of unease, wondering if he had triggered the chain of events.

"I was only being friendly and helpful on the first trip to the station but, if I'm totally honest …" He paused for a second and glanced down the hallway to see if Seraphina was anywhere near.

"I'm all ears, Mr Buchanan. Go on, please. I don't think your wife will hear you from here," smiled the inspector, as he tapped the thick walls.

"Call me Howard, please. Look, if I'm totally honest, I engineered the second meeting. Seraphina thinks I only helped Sarah once." He lowered his voice a little and continued, "That's because there's nothing really to tell. It was all perfectly innocent."

"I can see you feel pretty guilty about this, Howard, especially as it provoked such an angry response from her husband in the pub." The inspector checked his understanding. "So, you suggest it might be Mike, Sarah's husband, who smashed your window and wrote that threatening note?"

"Well, I can't think who else it might be! What do you think?"

"I can understand your concern, Howard," replied the inspector, as he spun around slowly on the office chair and took in his surroundings. He couldn't help but notice the many how-to instruction books scattered around the room, with barely any reading books in sight.

"It's difficult to say so soon. We'll need to investigate further to identify potential suspects," he continued with a calm and reassuring voice. "It's important that we keep an open mind and explore all possibilities. If you don't mind me asking, Howard, what sort of work are you looking for, now that you've given up city life?"

"A superb question indeed. Well, I haven't quite decided yet. I always thought I would know it when I saw it. Seraphina's not too impressed, though. She thought we would both have some time off when we moved here, but then she landed a job in the first couple of weeks. She works at the accountancy office just off the high street. As for me …"

He hesitated. Was this going to be the first person he told about his book-writing adventure? He decided it was probably best to, so that the inspector knew all the facts.

"Well, I have kept myself busy in the days with a small project of my own. First, I was busy with all the house renovations but, since then, I have occupied my time writing a book. Not a word to Seraphina, though! I've never done this before and don't know how it will pan out."

He looked at the inspector, keen to see his reaction.

His passion for writing intrigued the inspector. "That sounds fascinating. I've always fancied the idea of writing a good murder mystery myself, but I would be afraid of inadvertently including something from a real case and getting myself into trouble. So, tell me more about your writing. What's your book about?"

Howard's eyes lit up with excitement. "The story follows a retired detective who is called back into action when a body is found in the local library. He teams up with the librarian to solve the murder. They uncover a web of secrets, deceit, romance, and financial fraud, which leads back to the city, and all the lies threaten to tear a business apart."

The inspector's interest was piqued and he leaned forward. "That sounds like a fascinating story, Howard. I'd love to read it when it's finished. You'll have to keep me updated on your progress."

"I guess I'm writing about what I know, but not the fraud bit, obviously, Inspector!" and he suddenly felt like he had owned up to a crime he hadn't committed.

The inspector laughed, "Yes, okay, don't panic. I believe you."

Howard felt he needed to explain himself further and continued, "It's just something I've always wanted to try my hand at and I saw this as my chance. But you must promise not to tell Seraphina. It's not a big secret but, if I told her, she'd want to read it, critique it, edit it, and then tell everyone about it. She's a superb organiser, you see. I just want to do this by myself and see where it leads. It might all turn out to be rubbish but I'll never know unless I try. Seraphina thinks I'm being lazy by not looking for a job, but I need to give this a go first. You understand, don't you, Inspector?"

The inspector nodded sympathetically and replied, "I completely understand. Your secret's safe with me. Pursuing a dream can be daunting, especially when it's something new, and if you ever need a test reader, you're looking at one. Here, have one of my cards and let's hope you only use it to ring me when your book's finished. But back to the matter at hand. I'll check out this man you call Mike first thing in the morning. It's getting late now, so let's rejoin my DC and your wife."

He took one last twirl around in the chair before standing up and gesturing for Howard to go first. Howard felt relieved and grateful for the inspector's understanding as he led the way back down the hallway to the kitchen. When they arrived, they found Seraphina and the DC chatting away like old friends.

The inspector tapped Hicks on the shoulder and said, "Come on, it's been a long day and you still need to write all this up." Turning to Seraphina, he added, "Make sure Howard blocks up that window before you go to bed, won't you? Yesterday, I would have said that not much happens around here but, after the day I've had, I'm not so sure."

He made his way towards the front door, yawning as he went, followed by the DC.

"It was lovely to meet you, Seraphina, although I wish it was under better circumstances," said Hicks. "Maybe once this is all behind you, we could meet for coffee? I could show you that the village isn't such a terrible place to live."

"As soon as we know anything, we'll be in touch," said the inspector, reassuringly. "Try not to worry about it in the meantime and hopefully you will be able to get a good night's sleep."

The inspector and the DC left, leaving Howard to patch up the window.

"You go up to bed, and I'll be up shortly. I'm off to the shed to sort out something to block up this window." Seraphina didn't argue and went straight up to bed, feeling drained from the evening's events.

It was fortunate that the summer evenings stayed light until late, and Howard quickly found two leftover sheets of plywood from the renovation work. By the time he had finished, the pub was closing and he could hear cheers from a group of teenagers as they walked by at the end of the street.

As he stood back to admire his work, he thought he saw a movement out of the corner of his eye and spun around quickly to look. In the failing light, he thought he saw Sarah in the distance, but Charlie's bark distracted him. When he looked up again, there was no one there. He decided he must have been mistaken and dismissed it. Happy with his repair, he gathered up his tools and went inside. He locked the front door with all the bolts, then put Charlie to bed before going up to bed himself.

"How's the window looking?" asked Seraphina in a sleepy voice.

"I'm quite pleased with it. I sandwiched the window with two pieces of plywood and duct-taped them around the edges. Then, where there was no glass, I drilled some holes and screwed the two pieces together from the inside. Unless someone has a screwdriver with them, they won't be able to get through. If they try, Charlie will bark, so we're all safe. You can sleep well tonight, my love."

"Thank you. I suppose you're quite the handyman nowadays aren't you?"

Whilst he had been fixing the window, she had lain awake in bed, deep in thought. She had enjoyed her chat with the DC and, strangely, it had helped her put everything into perspective. She resolved to encourage and support Howard more, rather than constantly feel angry with him. And, as the DC had reminded her, they needed to stick together in times of trouble. She would try hard not to have her head turned by the likes of Ziggy, who must stop flirting with her. She would have a word with Chris on Monday. For now, she concluded that she would support her husband.

As Howard turned off the light to their ensuite and crossed the bedroom, Seraphina looked up at him. Amused, she said, "You've got toothpaste at the edge of your mouth."

Howard hopped into bed and, after he had wiped his face with the back of his hand, asked, "There, have I got it?"

Seraphina rolled over towards him and replied, "All gone now. Goodnight," as she snuggled up to him.

Taken aback by her display of affection, Howard lay with his arm around her, wondering what was going on in her head. One minute she was shouting at him, saying how much she hated it in the village and blaming it all on him and, the next minute, she was snuggling up close. Something had made an impact. Was it the brick through the window or the extended chat in the kitchen with the DC?

He said nothing. Whatever was going on in her head, he was sure that he would never work it out, but she would tell him in the end.

ELEVEN

Saturday early morning

Seraphina woke to the sound of Howard saying, "Cup of tea?"

She mumbled from beneath the covers, "Are you asking or offering?" Howard sat up in bed and replied, "I'm offering, and I'll check on the window at the same time." With a gentle voice, he continued, "I don't think we'll be able to visit Kew Gardens today, Sweetheart. We need to sort out the window."

Still sleepy, she responded, "No, you're probably right."

He made his way downstairs, while she snuggled down and drifted back off to sleep.

"Here you go, Sweetheart, a nice cup of tea, just as I promised," he said, as he placed the cup on the bedside table.

"You were quick!" Seraphina exclaimed as she shuffled up the bed to reach for her tea.

"I don't think so. I've already opened the curtains downstairs, let Charlie out, fed him his breakfast, and tidied up the kitchen from last night. Oh, and I've also got hold of a specialist glazier, who will be here in about twenty minutes. You must have nodded off again. Come on, Sleepyhead, drink your tea and let's figure out what we're doing today."

She sat up and took a sip of her tea. "Ew! it's almost cold!" she complained.

"Well, I made it a while ago. I'll make you another one in a minute. But first, we need to get dressed for the glazier, as he'll be here soon. You might be happy to greet him in your PJs but I'm not," Howard laughed.

"And maybe today we might even find out who smashed our window and, better still, why!" she said, hopefully.

Howard quickly got dressed, choosing a pair of dark blue jeans and a plain white T-shirt. He was halfway down the stairs when the doorbell rang. He rushed to open the door. "Good morning. I assume you're the glazier. You were quick!"

"Hi, yes. I'm Mark. We spoke on the phone," he said, offering his hand to Howard. "I'm fairly local. I knew where you were as soon as you said on the phone. I used to hang around in what would have been half of this house when I was a boy, as one of my old schoolmates used to live here. You mentioned on the phone that someone tossed a brick through your window. I know most people around here, so I might recognise who did it. Did you see them?"

"Unfortunately, not."

"That's a shame," said Mark, as he checked out the broken window and Howard's work. "For a quick patch-up in the dark, you've done pretty well. I looked at the windows outside before I rang your bell. As you said over the phone, your suspicions are correct. These windows aren't the sort you can instantly repair. Luckily, they're not original but a modern replica. It's an excellent copy, mind you, but at least we'll be able to mend them sooner rather than later."

"I thought they were the original!" said Howard, disappointed. "They looked original to me. I'm sure that's what the estate agent said when she showed us around!"

"The day an estate agent is an expert on windows is the day I retire," Mark replied. "It's like this, Howard. It all depends on how old you think 'old' is. I'd estimate these to be around one hundred years old. Whereas your house is a lot older. It would be better if I could repair this window, rather than trying to match up a new one, if that's okay with you?"

Mark waited for Howard's approval.

"Yes, I would prefer it to be repaired, if possible."

"Would you like a quote first? I feel like it won't be cheap," Mark asked as he made a note of the measurements.

"It's got to be done. You might as well get on with it."

"Okay then. I'll need to take the entire panel away. At least you made the house safe last night. That saved you a decent amount of money. Emergency call-out charges aren't cheap. I'll just get my tools from the van," he said, pointing at his vehicle, which was conveniently parked directly in front of the house.

"Can I make you a cup of tea or coffee?"

"Lovely, I'll have a nice strong tea please, with two sugars."

Howard was about to step out of the front door with Mark's tea when he saw Barbara walking briskly in his direction, pulling a shopping trolley behind her. As she got closer, she greeted him cheerfully, "Good morning, Howard. How nice to see you, and what do we have here?

You told me all the renovations were finished. New windows now, is it?"

"Morning, Barbara. No, not new windows. Just one that needs fixing. I think we will be the talk of the village for a while longer, though. You saw what happened on Thursday night at the pub, didn't you?"

She nodded, thrilled at the possibility of hearing some gossip first-hand. "Well, someone's only gone and thrown a brick through our window now."

"No! That's awful! Surely you don't think the two are connected?" Her inquisitive nature was triggered, and she looked keenly at Howard for a reply.

"Well, you'll find out soon enough, so you might as well hear it from the horse's mouth." She casually leaned over her shopping trolley, making herself comfy. Any rush she might have been in could wait.

"Well, we were both at home last night in the study when it happened. We rushed through and found that some, and I'm being polite here, 'person' had thrown a brick through our window with a note attached to it."

"Oh, my god, how awful," exclaimed Barbara. Desperate to know more, she couldn't stop herself from asking, "What did it say?"

"I thought you'd want to know. It said something about not being welcome here."

He watched as her eyes popped at his words. He was sure she would trot straight off to June and tell her all about it, which would inevitably sweep through the village like wildfire.

"I can't believe it. What's happening to this village? Never mind about the pub the other night. What about the murder yesterday? You don't think they're connected, do you? We've had no trouble in the village before, and now three things in a week." She paused just long enough to take a breath and then carried on talking at speed. "One thing's for sure, all the action seems to be around you," she said, raising her eyebrows and pointing her finger at him. "You take care now and try to have a good day. I must dash." She scurried off in the direction of the corner shop, leaving Howard to wonder what she would tell June.

Mark was busy securing the house from the inside when he stuck his head through the gap and asked, "Was that little old Mrs Barbara Wright?"

"Yes, it was."

"I haven't seen her in a while. She's lived here all her life. She may make out she's a timid little thing, but don't be fooled. There's nothing she doesn't know. Does she still work at the corner shop with June?"

"Yes, she does."

"You wouldn't know this but, a few years ago, me and the lads were in the local on a Saturday afternoon. We were sitting in the corner having a few beers, watching the rugby, as you do. In stormed this bloke asking the whole pub if anyone had seen his wife. Barbara and her husband were also there and seemed to know him. She only went and told him where his wife was, which would have been okay if she wasn't on her way to town with another fella! She said it so naturally. Barbara knew she was spilling the beans but calmly added that she'd just seen her walking to the train station with whatever his name was. She even had the nerve to say she thought they were going to town to catch a movie or something! The bloke was fuming and stormed out of the pub as fast as he came in. I don't know what happened next but I think it ended in divorce, and I can't say I've seen either of them since. Village life, eh? What do you make of it so far, Howard?"

"Well, it's interesting if nothing else, but I guess it takes some getting used to. I'm used to the anonymity of city life and I'm not sure if I'm keen on being the centre of attention." He logged everything Mark had said about Barbara. He could hardly believe she would do such a thing and was wishing she didn't know so much about his life.

Mark nodded in agreement. "Yes, it takes some getting used to, but it's a nice place really and the sense of community is strong here."

Keen to change the subject, Howard asked, "I see you're almost done. How long do you think it will take to repair?"

"I'll be in touch. If not on Monday, then definitely Tuesday. Hopefully, I'll also know the cost by then. I won't charge for the boarding today as I reused the plywood from last night and added a few security screws. No one will get in now."

He handed Howard his business card and continued, "My number is on the card, as well as my emergency number. You take care now and try to stay out of any more trouble. From what I overheard, it sounds like you've been having a rough time lately." He shook Howard's hand before leaving as quickly as he arrived.

Just then, Seraphina glided down the stairs, looking very smart, and asked, "Where's the glazier then?"

"He's done everything he can today. You missed him, messing around upstairs," he teased.

"I wasn't messing around. I was getting ready for the day. Anyway, I've been thinking. I reckon we should at least have a go at finding the coward that would rather throw a brick through our window than confront us! I think we should start at the corner shop, then head to the pub for a spot of lunch and make some subtle enquiries. This village won't break me. What do you think?" She had done some serious thinking while she was getting dressed and had concluded that she was determined not to be beaten.

"Blimey, Seraphina. What's got into you? I thought you hated this village." He was surprised at her change of attitude.

"Well, I was thinking. I do quite like my job, and we've spent a small fortune to get the house how we want it. I'm not prepared to be scared away by someone just because they think we're stepping on their toes. 'Not welcome here' - what sort of a message is that? It's a message from a coward, that's what it is. A coward that hasn't got the nerve to say it to our faces." She had found a renewed determination. She had never been a quitter and wasn't about to start.

"You know, Seraphina, you're absolutely right. Let's get out there and see what we can discover. I'm sure the inspector won't mind." Howard was always at his best when he had a determined and motivated wife behind him. He was thrilled she was back.

Seraphina continued, "You never know, we might meet some nice people as well. After all, they can't all be rotten, can they? Take that DC Hicks from last night. She was a very nice person and she's a local. Let's have some breakfast, then we can head out."

"Ah, so that's where you got your inspiration from. Were you two talking tactics last night then?" Howard joked, but he didn't mind as he was pleased that his old

Seraphina had returned. Now Sarah was the last thing on his mind.

"Right, breakfast it is, my love," said Howard, as they headed for the kitchen.

TWELVE

Saturday morning

When Barbara arrived at the corner shop, she could barely contain her excitement as she eagerly described her encounter with Howard to June. "And I'm sure it was Mark Smith I saw repairing the window. I haven't seen him for a while. He moved to the next village, if I recall correctly."

Barbara was in full flow, swinging from speculating about who smashed Howard's window to reminiscing about Mark, who had gone to school with her daughter. Reminiscing with June was one of Barbara's favourite pastimes, but they were soon interrupted as Sarah hobbled into the shop.

"Good morning, Sarah, how's the ankle today?" asked June.

"It's gradually getting better, thanks for asking. I'm quite good with these crutches now, although I have to keep telling myself it's not forever."

"You'll be mended before you know it. You're not normally here on a Saturday morning, are you? Is there something special you need?"

"Well, it's kind of doctor's orders, really. He said I should keep mobile, even though I might be tempted to sit around while I'm in plaster. So, I've taken his advice and

I've been going for random short walks. This morning I've come to get a magazine. It's just a shame I can't bring my dog, but with the crutches it's just too much. Mike's been awesome though, and he's been walking him for me."

"That's nice dear. That's what husbands are for, to look after you in times of need, aren't they?" June said, smiling.

"Yes, it is, but it means Mike's going short of sleep. Doing the early morning walk when he should go to bed. It can't be easy, bless him."

So that Barbara could hear everything, she occupied herself by filling up the chocolate counter, even though she wasn't working that morning. She couldn't help herself, as she asked, "I bet you've seen Howard's window this morning, then?" She knew full well that the route from Sarah's didn't include passing Howard's house.

"No, why? What's happened to his window?" Sarah asked sheepishly.

June looked at Barbara, a little annoyed that she was about to gossip in the shop, and said firmly, "Barbara, can you nip out the back and get me some more milk? I'm going to need it for the coffee."

Barbara looked up and was about to point out that she wasn't working but, when she saw the look June was giving her, she didn't argue and headed into the back to get the milk.

June looked at Sarah and lowered her voice. "She's a terrible busybody, isn't she? Don't you worry about Howard's window. It's nothing, I'm sure. Now, is that all you need this morning, Sarah dear?" Sarah nodded and paid June for the magazine.

"You have a lovely day," said June.

As soon as the door had closed, June turned to Barbara and asked, "Just what exactly do you think you're doing? Has it not occurred to you that it could have been Sarah's husband who put that brick through Howard's window?"

She was amazed at Barbara's lack of thought and continued, "After what happened in the pub the other evening, and now this, he's got to be the number one suspect."

Just as June said the word 'suspect', Inspector Southerby and DC Hicks entered the shop.

"Good morning, ladies. I wonder if you could spare us a few minutes of your valuable time for a little chat," asked the inspector, as he got out his wallet and showed his badge.

June took her glasses from the top of her head and put them on to read the inspector's name badge. She then twirled her glasses around in her hand and smiled gently at him.

"Oh, my word, Inspector Southerby. I thought it was you. I don't expect you to remember, but we met years ago when we had a burglary here at the shop. Gosh, that's got to be nearly 25 years ago. I was so much younger then," she said flirtatiously, as she popped her glasses back on her head, straightened her clothes, and fiddled with her hair. "You haven't changed at all! You were in uniform back then and now look, an inspector, fantastic. Can I get you a drink at all, a coffee maybe, Inspector?"

He smiled politely, oblivious to her flirtatious manner. "Oh yes. Well, nice to meet you again after all this time. We're here on official business, I'm afraid, but coffee would still be lovely. I take mine nice and milky, no sugar, thank you." He remained focused and continued, "We were hoping to ask you a few questions."

"No problem at all," replied June, as she turned to Hicks and asked, "Would you like a drink, my dear?"

"I'll have a latte, please."

The inspector looked at Hicks and rolled his eyes. He knew full well she had just ordered the same drink. He lowered his voice and said to her, "You're not making fun of my coffee again, are you, Hicks?"

"Me, Sir? Never, Sir," she quipped, as she smiled at him.

"Please, have a seat and I'll bring them over, sharpish. We can have a nice chat then," said June. She turned to Barbara, who was shuffling around the back of the counter rather sheepishly. June gave her a look that said, 'Stay where you are and keep your mouth shut!'

While the inspector waited, he noticed how well-organised and tidy the shop was. It was clear that June took pride in her business.

After setting the drinks down, she pulled up a chair and asked, "So, what can I do for you this morning, then? Don't tell me you've found my burglar after all this time."

"That was quite a few years ago. I was a young, keen officer back then. Sadly, we never caught the scoundrel who did it."

June was thrilled and exclaimed, "You do remember me then? How lovely." She smiled and moved a little closer to him. "And I remember you in your uniform. Very nice you looked too!" She flashed him a big smile and sat back in her chair, fiddling with her hair once again.

The inspector kept the conversation focused. "Anyway, I have a few questions about yesterday morning and the poor chap at the train station. I expect you've heard all about it." He produced a photograph of the victim and showed it to her, saying, "His name was Andrew Pankhurst. I'm led to believe he was known as Andy. Did you know him?"

June looked at the picture, and replied, "I've served him a few times with a drink or paper on the way to the station. Other than that, no. I know very little about him."

Barbara peered over the counter in a way that couldn't go unnoticed, and June felt guilty for scowling at her, having wrongly assumed that the police were coming to talk about Howard's window. She asked Barbara to join them. "Inspector, this is my friend and assistant, Barbara."

Turning to Barbara, she explained, "Look, the inspector has a photo here of the poor chap from the station yesterday. Come and see if you recognise him."

Barbara shuffled over as fast as her feet could carry her and studied the photo intently for ages before saying, "No, sorry, Inspector. As June says, I only know him from the few times he's called in here. So, what exactly happened then?"

The inspector quickly deduced that Barbara was the epitome of nosiness and decided she might be an asset in their investigations. "Barbara, was it? What's your surname, please?" as he indicated to Hicks to make a note of their names.

"Yes, my name is Barbara. Barbara Wright. And this is June, June Stoker, but it seems you two know each other already, anyway. I've worked for June for years."

"Right then Barbara and June. Is it okay if I call you by your first names?" he checked. They nodded enthusiastically, keen to hear what he was going to say next. "Good. I expect you both see and hear quite a lot in this shop. I would like you to be my eyes and ears on the street, please, if that's okay with you?"

Barbara looked thrilled, whilst June listened carefully.

"Now ladies, look, we know the victim used the train daily to commute to the city. We've had a look at the CCTV footage but it was so busy it's been hard to pick out any individual as everyone huddled, forming a crowd, as they rushed to board the train. It was only when the majority had boarded that this poor chap dropped to the ground, and a bystander helped."

He paused for a moment, allowing them time to process the information, and to see if they were going to say anything. Greeted with silence, he continued by asking, "How long have you lived in the village, Barbara?"

"Oh, forever," she replied and smiled kindly. "It's a lovely place to live. Everyone gets on so well. We have a great local pub and quite an active cricket and football team. I wouldn't want to live anywhere else."

June laughed, "You make it sound like something out of an old English fairy tale. You look at things through rose-tinted glasses sometimes, Barbara. You're forgetting all the grief poor old Howard's had lately." She trailed off, realising that she had just said more than she meant to, but the inspector was quick to inquire further.

"Who is Howard, and what bother has he had? Is there anything you would like to share, June?"

Hicks added, in a gentle but encouraging tone, "Yes, June. This is a murder investigation, so any information you have, no matter how irrelevant it may seem, can sometimes be important."

"Well, we had better close the shop for a moment then. I don't want my customers to think I'm gossiping. I'm sure it's not connected, Inspector, as Howard's such a nice chap!"

Barbara didn't need to be asked. She walked over to the door and swung the sign to read 'Closed'. Dropping the latch, she joined them at the table. Both ladies carefully recalled everything they could about Thursday night at the pub.

"That's quite a night you both had. Hicks, did you get that? The Coach and Horses," as he gestured to her to write it down, even though she had been making copious notes throughout their call. Unbeknown to June and Barbara, she was comparing their version of events with Seraphina's.

The inspector continued, "This curry and quiz night sounds like an exciting evening. Maybe I should take Mrs Southerby there sometime. Anyway, ladies, that's all for the time being. Thank you for your help. Oh, just one more thing. Would you mind if we got a quick photo of you both? Let me reassure you, this is quite the normal practice now. We do it to everyone we speak to on a murder enquiry, with their permission obviously. The photos are never distributed unless, of course, you turn out to be the murderer!" He laughed and continued, "I'm sure you're both innocent. Is that okay?"

June and Barbara looked at each other and nodded their heads. Standing up, they tried to find the best place to take the picture. Still enjoying his coffee, the inspector remained seated and turning to Hicks, asked, "Can you get a quick picture of the ladies, please? Anywhere. Location is not important."

She was already up and tried to zoom in with her phone as they started fussing with their hair. Like a couple of schoolgirls, they tried to glimpse their reflection in the shop window.

"No need for perfection, ladies. It's not a portrait, just a quick reminder. You both look lovely anyway," she said, trying to calm them.

"Oh, Inspector, what must you think of me? I'm such a fusspot," said June, looking over at him and winking.

"Right. Please turn to me, ladies and give me a quick smile if you will," said Hicks, snapping away as fast as she could.

"Is that on your phone, Dear? Can I have a look?" asked June.

Hicks laughed and replied, "It's not for the family album you know but, if you insist, here you go, if it puts your mind at rest. Just like I said, you both look lovely."

June and Barbara had a quick preview, sharply interrupted by the inspector, "Come on, ladies. You're not entering a beauty contest!"

He finished his drink and left the table. "Here, take one of my cards. If you see or hear anything that may be of use, please don't hesitate to give me a ring." Pulling them back to the stark reality of the murder investigation, he handed them each a card.

Noticing their concerned expressions, he attempted to reassure them. "Try not to worry too much, ladies. I'm sure we'll have everything sorted and the murderer behind bars soon. And thank you for the coffee. How much do we owe you?"

June spun around quickly, suddenly remembering that she had closed the shop. "Don't worry about that. For you, it's free today. Here, let me get the door." She hurried over to open it and, as the inspector passed, she leaned forward and said, "I hope you don't take me for someone who gossips."

He turned to face her. "Don't worry. You've both been very helpful."

June was deeply concerned as she hated to be perceived as one who spread gossip. She strived to maintain her reputation as a trustworthy shopkeeper who could keep a confidence, unlike some village residents. She was thankful that no customers had called while the police were there.

She turned to Barbara and said, "Now, look, we must keep our eyes and ears open, as the inspector said. But I don't want you to mention to anyone about the police being here. It might deter customers from coming in. Do you understand?"

"What about Ian? Can I tell him?"

"Of course, you can tell your husband, but please ask him not to tell anyone else. There's still a murderer at large and it could be anyone. Goodness, we might even know them!"

The inspector and Hicks left the shop and walked to the car in silence. Once inside, they could speak without being overheard. Hicks began. "It was good to get another perspective on Thursday night's events but essentially it all tallied up with my notes just maybe a little more detail."

"Yes, having multiple statements about an event is always beneficial. These ladies seem to observe more than they realise. We should check in with them over the next few days. While I think about it, can you organise a stand at the train station first thing on Monday? Get some uniforms there to talk to the regular commuters. Let's find out if anyone knows anything or, better still, saw anything."

"Good idea, Sir. I'll get that sorted. A reassuring police presence is always a good idea, anyway. Oh yes. I liked the way you mentioned your wife when we were in there." She couldn't hide the smirk on her face as she teased him. "That June seemed a little keen on you, didn't she, Sir?"

"What can I say?" he laughed. "I'm a good-looking guy. But you can stop with your suggestions, Hicks. Just drive."

THIRTEEN

Saturday mid-morning

The village no longer had a police station, so the inspector and Hicks were based a short 20-minute drive away, in the nearest town.

It was an old Victorian building with beautifully coloured stained-glass windows. Inside, the rooms had intricate plaster coving and mouldings which decorated the ceilings. It all seemed a million miles away from the modern office technology that they used nowadays.

As they entered the incident room, they could see three transparent perspex screens already covered in post-it notes. One had the usual collection of photographs and arrows, identifying who was who, with information about any possible connections. Another had a map detailing the victim's last known route, and a third screen headed 'SUSPECTS' was looking very empty. As the sun beamed in through the tall leaded windows, the stained-glass windows cast red and green shadows over the room.

Hicks added the photos of June and Barbara and stared at the incident boards, contemplating the puzzling case. She turned to the inspector and shared her thoughts. "I've been trying to think why anyone would target an innocent commuter. According to what we've gathered so far, he's not married, has no children that we know of, and both his parents have already passed away. Bit of a private chap from all accounts."

"Get that up on the board, Hicks. If we're talking about it, then it's a material fact and needs to be noted. What else do we have?"

They studied the boards together for what seemed like an age.

This was only the second murder investigation Hicks had been assigned to. Her first case was a cut-and-dry classic, with the husband killing his wife in a rage of temper. She felt that she could cut her teeth on this murder if only she had a clue as to who did it. Eventually, she broke the silence of concentration, declaring, "Right, I've got nothing. I'm going to get a coffee. Can I get you one, Sir?"

"Yes, Hicks, that would be great. Thanks."

The inspector was a gentle sort. He had a manner about him that, when he spoke, his comforting voice immediately calmed people down. He made them feel that everything was going to be okay, whatever the situation. The calmness that comes with maturity was just what Hicks needed and she was glad to have him as her boss and mentor. When she returned with two coffees, she found that he had arranged the boards in a straight line and was sitting directly in front of them.

"Any thoughts yet, Sir?" she asked as she passed him his coffee.

"Well, not yet. I often find if I just sit awhile, something often comes to me. Why don't you try it?" he said, as he grabbed another chair from one of the nearby desks and put it next to his. He patted the seat with his hand. "Come on, don't be shy. You give it a go. See if you can come up with anything. Best hope that the chief doesn't catch us though or he'll think we're doing nothing."

It was too late. The door flew open and in marched Chief Super Intendant Carrol. He was a tall man, with a very full head of thick black hair and had a habit of running his hands through it from front to back. With his very clear public-school English accent, he saw himself as a 'bit of a Hugh Grant'. Like Hicks, he was quite new to the role, having recently been promoted from a London borough, and was keen to make an impact.

"Morning, morning. What are you doing, Southerby, sitting there drinking coffee when we have a murderer on the loose?"

The inspector turned round and calmly announced, "Ah, morning, Chief. How nice to see you. Well, what with you coming from the city, you'll be up to date with all the latest techniques, I'm sure."

The chief half-smiled and let him continue. "Maybe you would like to join us. We're just about to go through the Abraham Theory to see if we can move this case forward."

"Ah, well, very good. I was just popping in to show my face. I'm sure you've got it covered. You carry on and show Hicks how it's done, won't you? Keep me up to date with your progress. If you need any more people on the case, see me." He made a swift exit, looking like he had somewhere more important to be.

"As I was saying, before we were so rudely interrupted, come and sit next to me and have a look at this board."

Hicks took a seat, and they both stared at the incident board while they sipped their very hot machine-made coffee. She waited for him to say something, but the only sound to break the silence was the occasional phone ringing in the background.

Eventually, the inspector jumped up, rushed across the room and grabbed a thick black dry-wipe pen. Heading directly to the 'SUSPECTS' board, he turned to her and asked, "What's missing, Hicks? What's missing?"

She looked at him blankly, trying to think of something smart or clever to say but, in reality, she was still trying to work out what the Abraham Theory was. She had nothing constructive to add. Instead, she shrugged her shoulders and looked at him for inspiration.

He turned to the empty 'SUSPECTS' board and added the word 'MOTIVE' in capital letters before circling it. Returning to his seat, he continued to sit silently, looking at the boards. After a few moments, he threw his hands in the air and exclaimed, "Well, I've got nothing either, not even a suspicion. Can you see any connections?"

Hicks was relieved, pleased to know it wasn't just her. "No, Sir. But, to be honest, I've been sitting here waiting for you to enlighten me about this Abraham Theory."

The inspector burst out laughing. "There isn't one. I just made it up, to get that jumped-up know-it-all youngster of a chief out of my office, and he fell for it!" He chuckled to himself.

"What does that make me then, Sir? I fell for it too! I don't know if I should be offended."

"Now then, Hicks, calm down. You asked, didn't you? He didn't! Anyway, I didn't have you down as one of those cotton-bud generation people you talk about."

Trying to keep a straight face, she asked, "Do you mean snowflake, Sir?"

"You're not taking the mickey out of me again, are you, Hicks?" he said, as he looked sideways at her, half-smirking.

Hicks gave her usual reply. "Me, Sir? Never, Sir." Both smiling, they looked at each other silently and acknowledged a draw.

The inspector ran back over what they knew, recapping out loud. "Back to the drawing board. What can it tell us? I see uniform have interviewed the victim's work colleagues, and everyone there seems to have an alibi that checks out so, I guess for the moment, we'll assume they're all telling the truth."

"Should we focus our search on someone closer to home then maybe? Shame he doesn't have a wife. It usually turns out to be the spouse in murder cases, doesn't it?" asked Hicks, with an excited tone of voice. She was enjoying herself, despite the long day yesterday and the early start today.

"Well, as right as you might be, he doesn't have a wife, and no girlfriend has popped up yet either. Who do you think we should visit next, Hicks?"

"Well, I am struggling to see any connections at all at the moment."

Just then, she had an inspired thought and said, "I am wondering though, what if it might be exactly what I said earlier, Sir?"

"What exactly did you say earlier?" He was intrigued by what she meant.

"Earlier, when we first came in. I said, 'Why would anyone want to target an innocent commuter?' Well, maybe that's exactly what it was. A case of mistaken identity! And, if that's the case, does that mean we should expect another murder? I'm probably wrong, but it's just a thought."

The inspector said nothing. Instead, he continued to sit in silence, looking at the board for a little while longer. Eventually, he spoke. "Hicks, that's not outside the realm of possibility. Stranger things have happened." He stood up and wrote on the board 'Mistaken Identity?' and put it in a bubble. Then he checked with her, "Have you sorted it with uniform to be at the station on Monday morning?"

"Yes, I've also arranged for them to be there for the evening returns, in case they miss some in the morning rush."

"Good. Well, looking closer to home is what we're going to do today then. I think we should start by having a pub lunch. It's where most things seem to happen in that village. Please make sure I save the receipt though, investigative expenses, you know. Don't let me forget again, will you?" He was notorious for losing his receipts. After he lost all of last month's expenses, he vowed it would never happen again. "The Coach and Horses, isn't it?"

"Yes, Sir, it is. Sounds good to me. I'll get my bag and jacket," she replied enthusiastically.

"Go on then, I'll let you get the car as well, and I'll see you out the front."

FOURTEEN

Saturday mid-morning

Since it was one of Mike's few weekends off, he was determined to make the most of it. Being a lovely summer's day, he had got up early and taken Teddy, their dog, for an extra-long walk before the heat of the day set in.

"Hi, Sarah, we're back," he called as they arrived home. Their home was an old farmworkers' cottage on the fringe of the village, small but full of charm. Despite its size, it held a special place in his heart as he had lived there all his life, inheriting it from his mother when she passed away. Not long afterwards, he and Sarah had married.

Sarah's arrival brought a fresh perspective to the house, which had remained mostly unchanged since he was a child. Room by room, she had cleared out the tired old decor and replaced it with a classic country style, much like the one she wrote about in the magazine she worked for. She had thoughtfully placed each item with purpose and no sign of clutter. Much like the way she presented herself.

Mike looked through from the kitchen and saw Sarah sitting on the sofa, flicking through a new magazine. He called to her as he picked up the kettle. "It's a lovely day out there today. Teddy just ran and ran. Do you want a cup of tea?"

She looked affectionately at Teddy as he strolled into the living room and settled down on the rug in front of her. As she shifted her leg forward with some difficulty, so she could stroke him, she replied, "He looks like he's had a good workout. I'd love a cup of tea if you're making one."

Mike was quick with the drinks, and carefully placed the tray down on the side table next to her. "How are you feeling today, Sweetheart?"

"Oh, I'm fine. Just a little bored. Not being able to get around much has got me down a bit."

Mike reached into his pocket and pulled out a packet of painkillers and Sarah's regularly prescribed tablets. "Here you go," he said, handing them to her. "I brought these through for you as well. It doesn't look like you've taken your tablets today."

Sarah snapped back, "I don't need those tablets. It's my ankle, not my head." She continued to protest. "I don't need those drugs. There's nothing wrong with me!"

Mike paused for a moment as he studied her expression. He could see she felt down and he just wanted her to be happy. Mustering his most cheerful voice, he asked, "Right then, what about lunch? What do you fancy? Soup, a sandwich, or something more substantial? Or we could make a picnic and go down to the river? It's a beautiful day outside. I think it would do us both good to get some fresh air."

"As it's your weekend off, why don't you take me to the pub for lunch? Please?" She looked up at him and pleaded with her big eyes.

Mike searched for inspiration in the kitchen cupboards while considering her suggestion. After Thursday night, he wasn't keen to return so soon. The suggestion of a pub lunch reminded him of his encounter with Howard, and how she had happily accepted Howard's help. But each time Mike offered, she had declined and became increasingly stubborn and independently-minded, despite her happiness always lying at the heart of everything he did.

He desperately tried to think of a good reason not to go to the pub. He returned to the living room and sat next to her on the sofa, and said, "You've heard there's some dagger-wielding killer on the loose, haven't you?" He hoped this would be enough to dissuade her.

"Yes, and at the train station too. I must have only just missed it. But I'm sure we'll be fine. You'll be with me, and I always feel safe when you're around. Come on Mike, it'll make a pleasant change, I hardly ever go there." She threw him a smile which she knew would work its magic. He weakened, unable to refuse her a second time.

It was her smile that had caught his eye when she first walked into his classroom when they were both six years old. The teacher introduced her as 'the new girl' and asked for a volunteer to be her buddy. Mike had eagerly raised his hand and the boys had laughed at him. The teacher explained that she was looking for a female volunteer. Undeterred, and struck by Sarah's smile and beauty, he had looked out for her from that moment on. As an adult, Mike often thought to himself, 'Who's laughing now?' when he saw his former classmates in the pub with their broken marriages, lies and affairs.

He relented. "OK then, but I'll drive. I know it's not far, but I can see you've already been out for a walk this morning, and I don't want you to overdo it." He pointed to the magazine she had been reading, which could only have come from the corner shop.

"I know, I know, but I felt I was going stir crazy, and the doctor said I should keep mobile. Going back to work this week made me realise how insular I've become since I broke my ankle. Come on Mike, it'll be such a nice change." She reached for her crutches without touching the tea he had made her, or her tablets. "Can you pass me my handbag, please? I'll just check my face and hair. Are you going like that?" She was pleased to have won him over.

Mike and Sarah seemed like an odd match to most people, even when it came to their appearance. He preferred a more casual look and was mostly seen out in a pair of worn-out jeans and a T-shirt, while she was always impeccably dressed.

Mike walked over to the hallway mirror and looked himself up and down. "It's only lunch at the local. This'll be fine. Look, I'll bring the truck closer to the house and I'll see you out the front, okay?"

Although it was only a short drive to the pub, he didn't want Sarah to struggle on her crutches. He waited for her to reply but, as she was busy applying her lipstick, she gave him the thumbs-up sign to show her approval.

She didn't have to wait long before he pulled up right in front of the house. He hopped out of the cab and offered to help. It was one of those half-car half-truck vehicles, and the cab was quite high. Sarah insisted she could climb up into the passenger seat herself and, after some effort, she succeeded. All he could do was stand by and watch, ready to catch her if she stumbled. "You know, it would have been a lot easier if only you would let me help you. Are you comfy now?"

She took pride in her achievement. "Yes, I'm all good, thanks. You know I like to do things for myself."

When they arrived, she continued with her independent approach, refusing Mike's help. Instead, he walked slowly behind, ready to catch her if she stumbled. Once he had made sure she was comfortably seated in the beer garden, he headed off to the bar for drinks and a menu.

Debbie, the landlady, was behind the bar and greeted him cheerfully. "Hello, Mike. How nice to see you out with Sarah. Is it your weekend off?"

"Yes, it is," he replied, as he quickly scanned the lounge bar to see who was in before ordering the drinks. "I'll have a shandy, please, and a glass of white wine for Sarah."

It was unusual for Debbie to get a full sentence from him. His usual technique was to point to the pump in silence, and gesture for a pint. She wondered if maybe he was on his best behaviour after Thursday evening's events, or maybe it was because he had Sarah with him.

"I'll have a menu as well, please," asked Mike, almost forgetting. Debbie wondered if it was a special occasion. As far as she could remember, Mike and Sarah had only eaten in the pub together a handful of times in all the years they'd been married. She didn't like to pry though and replied, "Here are a couple of menus, and I'll bring your drinks over. In the meantime, the 'Today's Specials' board is over there." She pointed to the far wall.

Mike reached for his wallet. "How much?"

"Don't worry about that now. You can pay for everything when you've finished your meal. After all, it's not like I don't know where you live!" she said and smiled at him. He took the menus and joined Sarah in the sunshine.

Meanwhile, DC Hicks and Inspector Southerby had just finished their lunch.

"I'll just pop up to the bar and pay shall I, Sir?"

"Yes, and don't forget to get a receipt, will you?" he asked, handing her some cash. DC Hicks swiftly took Mike's place at the bar and caught Debbie's attention. As she waited for the change, she looked over to the beer garden where Sarah and Mike were sitting. He resembled the 'Mike' everyone had been talking to her about.

"Your change," announced Debbie.

"Oh, yes, thank you. We really enjoyed our meals. I hope you don't mind me asking, but can you please tell me who those people are that have just arrived?"

"Well, I'm not at liberty to say, I guess it depends on who's asking," replied Debbie, as she stood back and crossed her arms.

Hicks gave a quick flash of her badge. Immediately, Debbie leaned in closer. "I'm so sorry, it's just that I don't like to talk about people, you know what I mean. Why do you ask?"

Hicks replied, "Now that's where I'm not at liberty to say either," and smiled. "It's nothing interesting, I can assure you. I think they might be able to help me with some enquiries, that's all. Do you know their names, please?"

In a low voice, Debbie replied, "That's Mike and his wife, Sarah. They live in the end cottage on the way out of the village."

"Tennant? Mike and Sarah Tennant?" double-checked Hicks.

"Yes, that's right."

"Okay. Thanks very much, and thanks again for a lovely meal. Hopefully, I'll see you again soon, when I'm not at work," said Hicks, as she gave Debbie a reassuring smile. She was about to return to the inspector when she realised it might be a good idea to get Debbie's point of view about Thursday night's events. "Actually, I wouldn't mind talking to you about something, if that's okay. When's the best time to speak to you privately?"

"Oh really? Is that in a professional capacity?" Debbie suddenly felt a little nervous.

"Yes. Don't panic. It's only a couple of questions, but you look a little busy at the moment."

Debbie wondered if other customers knew who Hicks was. As a landlady, she didn't want to be seen talking to the police as she knew how suspicious some locals could be. Keeping her voice low, she replied nervously, "Later would be better, and please use the side door when you call."

"Great. Hopefully I'll see you later then," Hicks replied, before she headed back to report her plans to the inspector. As she sat down opposite him, he said, "You took ages. Did you get me a receipt?"

"Damn, no, I forgot! But, on the plus side, I have arranged to come back and see the landlady later. I thought it would be a good idea to get another point of view about the scuffle on Thursday night. What do you think, Sir?"

"One job. I gave you one job!" he laughed.

"Not to worry, Sir. I can get your receipt later when I come back, but you'll never guess who's out there in the beer garden," she said enthusiastically.

He paused for a second and she jumped in, not allowing him time to reply. "It's Mike and Sarah Tennant. That's saved us a trip, hasn't it, Sir?" She was pleased with her successful detective work and waited for an acknowledgement. But he said nothing and sat back in his chair, looking over to watch Mike and Sarah chatting in the beer garden and enjoying the sun.

"Oh, I see. You're going to let them finish their meal before speaking to them. That's kind Sir."

"No, I'm going to sit back and watch them discreetly from a distance. When they've finished, we'll follow them, hopefully they'll be going home. Then we'll give them ten minutes to get settled, before we visit them in private. From what I can see, they seem like a nice couple, not like the angry chap who had a go at Mr Buchanan. There are always two sides to every story, Hicks; always two sides. To be honest, I'd like to talk to the landlady before we speak to them, but I guess you've made a plan now, so we'll stick to it."

He calmly delivered the agenda, without criticism, but Hicks still felt slightly corrected. What he said made perfect sense and she nodded in agreement.

"Do you want me to change the time with the landlady, Sir?"

"No need, as we don't want to draw attention to ourselves. Let's see how things pan out here. I've often found observing people can be very informative. People's actions always give away more than you would credit. Watch and learn, Hicks, watch and learn."

She lifted their empty glasses. "I guess we'll have another one then. I'll have a coffee. What would you like, Sir?" He smiled and replied, "Make mine a tonic water, I'll just pretend it's got a shot of gin in it!"

Debbie returned to the bar with Mike and Sarah's order and found a growing queue of customers. Shouting through the kitchen, help arrived in the form of Cassie, Barbara's daughter. Cassie had been working the Saturday afternoon shift for about a month but, despite instruction from Debbie, she seemed to spend more time in the kitchen than in the bar.

Debbie sternly issued clear instructions to her. "Take this order to the kitchen, then come back quickly and collect the empties." She then turned to face the customers and instantly replaced her stern expression with a smile. Cheerfully, she called out, "Who's next, please?"

Hicks ordered the extra drinks and returned with them to their table. She and the inspector stretched them out for a pleasant hour or so, while Mike and Sarah enjoyed their lunch in the sun.

"I doubt whether they'll be much longer, Sir," said Hicks, just as Howard and Seraphina walked in. Trying not to be seen, they shuffled slightly to the left, partially shielding themselves with the exposed wood beams and joists that formed the main support for the old pub.

Seraphina marched up to the bar and confidently ordered two drinks, then turned to look at the 'Specials' board and asked Howard, "What shall we have to eat?"

Meanwhile, Howard had spotted Mike and Sarah in the beer garden and, as he turned his back to them, he noticed the inspector and Hicks. He wondered what they had walked into. It was on the tip of his tongue to suggest that they eat somewhere else when Seraphina saw them too.

Enthusiastically, she announced, "Look, Howard, there's that lovely DC Hicks and the inspector. She was so nice yesterday. Let's say hello." She didn't wait for his reply before she picked up their drinks from the bar and made a beeline over to their table.

"How nice to see you. Can we get you a drink?" she offered, as she waved their drinks in the air. "Are you on a stakeout, or maybe just having some steak out?" she asked, laughing loudly at her own joke. The inspector looked pained, and Seraphina noticed Hicks raise her eyebrows. "Oh, no, I'm interrupting, aren't I? I'm so sorry. We'll leave you in peace," Seraphina apologised.

The inspector stood up and said quietly, "Don't worry, Mrs Buchanan, but may I politely suggest that you avoid the beer garden on this particular visit, thank you. As soon as we know anything about your window, we'll be in touch."

His polite, yet firm demeanour commanded a natural authority that Hicks admired and longed to emulate. After successfully and politely dismissing Howard and Seraphina, he reclaimed his anonymous position.

As Seraphina turned to see what the inspector meant, she glimpsed Mike in the beer garden. Before she could react, Howard put his arms firmly around her shoulders and guided her to the other side of the pub.

"Come on, Seraphina," he whispered gently. "The last thing we need is trouble three days in a row." Although she was reluctant to sit indoors on such a beautiful day, she allowed Howard to choose a table. Despite her curiosity, she knew he was right. It probably was best to avoid any potential trouble.

Debbie didn't miss a thing and called out to them as they passed the end of the bar. "I'll bring the menus over to you in a moment, shall I?"

Howard looked over his shoulder and smiled at Debbie, nodding his head as he continued guiding Seraphina to a table.

Immediately after they had taken their seats, Seraphina turned to Howard and exclaimed, "Blimey, you couldn't make this stuff up, could you? I wonder who else might come in. It's quite exciting, isn't it?" Today, she was undeniably full of energy and determination. She had decided that they had as much right to be in the village as anyone else. In restoring an old village property, they had contributed to the ongoing success of several small local businesses and, as far as she was concerned, no one was going to tell her she didn't belong there, or get the better of her.

Cassie shuffled her way across the bar to deliver the menus, and asked, "Would you like any more drinks while you decide what to have?"

Howard looked up at Cassie and asked, "I hope you don't mind me prying, but are you Barbara's daughter by any chance? Barbara from the corner shop."

She replied, "Yes I am. How did you know? And please don't say I look like her!" as she rolled her eyes. Tempted as Howard was to say 'yes', he replied, "I thought so. I saw you with her at the 'Curry and Quiz' night. You were part of June's winning team, weren't you?"

Relieved not to be compared to her mother, she replied, "Oh I see. Yes, that's me, all brains. I've just realised who you are. You're that guy that Mike had a go at, aren't you? You know he's out there now with his wife, Sarah. You want to be careful he doesn't start again!"

Howard thought to himself how she not only looked like her mother but sounded like her too.

Seraphina responded with a patronising tone, "I think we can manage, my dear. We'll both have lasagne and the same drinks as before. Debbie knows what we had." She handed the menus back to Cassie in a dismissive manner. "That will be all for now, thank you."

As soon as Cassie returned to the bar, Debbie spoke to her firmly. "I've told you before not to gossip with the customers. Now, take that order to the chef."

Seraphina and Howard watched Debbie, who noticed them looking at her. She raised her hands in an apologetic gesture and mouthed, "Sorry."

Seraphina smiled at Howard. "This is funny, isn't it? She's such a busybody; just like you've described her mum. When she brings the food, I'll tell her about our window. People like that can't stop themselves from spreading, I mean, *sharing* information!" She found the whole situation amusing and planned to use it to her advantage by giving Cassie something to talk about.

The inspector and Hicks sat back and observed everything unfold. Meanwhile, Sarah and Mike were just finishing their meal as Cassie passed to collect their empty glasses. Mike asked for the bill, so she headed back to the bar to fetch it. As she reached over the bar for it, Debbie interrupted by saying, "I'll handle that, don't you think?"

Debbie grabbed the card machine from the bar and went out to their table. "I hope you enjoyed your meals. It's lovely to see you, Sarah. We don't see you here often enough." Smiling at Mike she passed him the bill.

Sarah looked up shyly and remained silent, as Mike paid in cash and said, "Thanks, keep the change."

Debbie sensed they weren't in the mood to chat and simply replied, "Thanks very much. Enjoy the rest of your day."

Mike stood up to help Sarah make her way to the truck, but she snapped at him sharply and loud enough for all to hear, "I can do this myself, thank you."

There was a momentary lull in the general chitchat as everyone watched her make her way to the truck, using her crutches, with no help from Mike.

Mike didn't appreciate it when Sarah caused scenes in public, but he opted to keep quiet. He knew it wasn't wise to engage in a debate with her at the pub, and no one would understand his perspective. As he closed the truck door, the pub chatter started up again with renewed vigour.

"Look, listen, and learn," said the inspector again.

Meanwhile, Seraphina had a good view of the car park from her window seat, but sitting just a little too far away she wasn't able to hear what was said. She could only see how Sarah struggled to get into Mike's truck, unaided. "Oh my God!" she exclaimed. "Howard, this place is unbelievable! He didn't help her at all. Why did he even bring her out for a meal if he had no plans to help her?" At that moment, she completely forgave Howard. While he felt deeply sorry for Sarah, he was relieved that Seraphina had finally calmed down.

"That was lucky," piped up Cassie, as she swung past Howard to collect their empties. "Mike didn't even realise you two were here, did he?" She couldn't stop herself from commenting as she passed by, but Seraphina called her back, quickly changing her tone from earlier. "Excuse me. Cassie, is it? Nice to meet you. I suppose you've heard what happened to our window last night, then?"

"Oh yes, it's awful, isn't it?" she replied, as she placed all the glasses she had collected on their table and pulled up a stool. "Mum told me earlier. Who do you think did it then? My money's on Mike if you ask me!"

Seraphina encouraged her to keep her eyes and ears open. "If you hear anything, we'd really appreciate it, wouldn't we, Howard?"

Cassie was happy to continue the conversation, but Debbie spotted her and called out sharply, "Glasses, Cassie, glasses!" She immediately jumped up and scurried off, just like her mother would. Howard chuckled to himself as he watched her go and made a mental note to include a character like her in a future book.

Seraphina looked at Howard. "Why are you grinning and what are you thinking?"

It was on the tip of his tongue to let her in on his dream of being an author, just as the inspector and Hicks walked up to their table.

"Hello, again. Now that our 'company' has left the premises, I just wanted to come over and apologise for my shortness earlier on. I hope it didn't spoil your meal," said the inspector.

Howard replied, "Oh, no worries, we totally understand. And lunch was lovely."

Seraphina continued in a strong, confident manner, "Yes, lunch was great, thanks. Look, Inspector, last night I was in shock, but I'm not anymore and I'm determined to get to the bottom of this window business."

"Well, it's good you're not frightened by last night's events, but please be sure to leave the policing up to us, won't you?" replied the inspector in a kind, but authoritative tone.

"Of course, and if I hear anything, Inspector, I'll let you know," she replied.

Still firm but reassuringly, the inspector said, "Well, hopefully, we'll be in touch with you first."

"Enjoy the rest of your weekend," added Hicks before they left.

As the doors of the inspector's car closed, he announced, "Right then, onwards to the Tennants' house. Hopefully, they've gone straight home."

FIFTEEN

Saturday early afternoon

The inspector checked his notepad and read aloud, "The last cottage before we leave the village. Yes, this looks like the place. Hicks, pull up here, please."

As they approached, they heard raised voices. Hicks and the inspector exchanged a look, wondering what they had stumbled upon. As they got closer, a man's voice shouted, "You can't just walk off without telling me!"

"That's coming from the Tennants' cottage," said Hicks. "Should I knock now, or shall we wait and see if it stops first, Sir?" Before the inspector could decide, they heard a smashing sound and a woman's voice shouting wildly, "I don't need them!"

As they stood on the doorstep, listening to the commotion, the front door partly opened to reveal Mike, with his back to them. Unaware of the visitors behind him, Mike yelled into the cottage, "Now, you just stay there until I get back!"

He spun around quickly, nearly knocking Hicks over. She could see the panic in his eyes, and she took a deep breath, uncertain of her next move. Despite the cottage's charming exterior, the sounds they could hear indicated that the inside might be far from idyllic.

Mike shouted at the DC as he stepped back into the doorway. "What the hell! What are you doing here?" He was visibly agitated and didn't allow Hicks to speak before he continued, "How long have you been here?"

The inspector calmly raised his badge and replied, "Questions, questions. I thought that was my job. It is Mr Tennant, isn't it? May we come in? Is now a good time?"

Mike sighed before replying sharply, "Yes, I'm Mike Tennant and no, it's not ideal at all. Do I have a choice?"

The inspector paused as he considered the options. "There is always a choice, Mr Tennant. We can talk here or we can talk down at the station." His calm composed manner in dealing with situations impressed Hicks. She knew she had much to learn from him and watched as Mike hesitated before replying. Finally, he relented. "You'd better come in then. I'm tight on time though," he said, as he ushered them quickly into the living room.

Sarah was sitting in the armchair and, as Hicks and the inspector entered the room, she reached for her crutches to stand up. Hicks quickly stopped her. "No need to get up on our account. It's Mr Tennant we wanted to speak to," she said, giving Sarah a warm smile.

"You can say anything in front of my wife," Mike replied defensively. "We have no secrets from each other."

"Very well, Sir," Hicks replied, holding up her badge. "I'm Detective Constable Hicks and this is Inspector Southerby. We'd like to ask you about an incident that occurred yesterday evening."

"Please, have a seat," Sarah offered, gesturing towards the sofa.

Hicks looked around the room, taking in the cosy and inviting atmosphere, and commented as she sat down,

"What a beautiful place you have here. It's lovely and homely."

The inspector cut in, aware that Mike had already said he was short on time. "I'll get straight to the point, if I may. We had a report of a brick being thrown through the window of a residential property and wondered if you know anything about it."

"I don't know what you're talking about," Mike replied, warily. "Where was this?"

The inspector didn't answer his question, but continued, "In that case, Mr Tennant, you wouldn't mind if we took your fingerprints to eliminate you from our inquiries, would you?"

Mike argued back, "Why do I need to be eliminated from your inquiries if I've done nothing wrong? You could at least tell me whose house it is!"

Hicks spoke up. "Yes Sir, the property belongs to a Mr Buchanan," she announced, as she watched closely for his reaction. Acutely aware of the time, Mike checked his watch before replying. "Well then, that's simple. I don't know any Mr Buchanan, let alone anything about a brick being thrown through his bloody window. When was this, anyway?"

Mike was becoming increasingly anxious. Despite Sarah believing she didn't need the medication, he knew all too well that it had caused their argument. A few moments earlier, she had flushed her pills down the toilet in a fit of temper. It wasn't the first time she had done that and he was worried about the consequences. It was crucial that he made it to the chemist before they closed for the weekend.

Sensing there was more to the situation, the inspector pushed a little further. "Maybe it would help if I were to tell you that the gentleman you were seen, shall we say, talking to in The Coach and Horses on Thursday evening was Mr Buchanan. Maybe now you can see the connection and understand the reason for our visit."

Sarah stared at Mike; her eyes widened with alarm. "What have you done, and who is Mr Buchanan anyway?"

Mike turned to Sarah and his expression softened. "I was just looking out for you," he said.

The inspector stepped in. He had a calm tone yet spoke with a confident authority. "Maybe a cup of tea would help," he suggested and gestured towards the kitchen. "Shall we go this way, Mr Tennant?"

Mike looked visibly disheartened as he silently walked to the kitchen. The inspector followed closely behind and, as he quickly scanned the room, he found the cause of the earlier smashing sound. Broken glass lay scattered across the kitchen worktop and sink.

"Mind yourself on that, won't you?" warned the inspector, as he pointed to it. Mike reached out for a dustpan and brush from a peg on the wall nearby. He cleared the shattered glass in silence and began to organise the drinks.

The inspector maintained a gentle tone as he continued with his questions. "So, you're not denying that you told Mr Buchanan to stay away from your wife on Thursday evening, then?

Mike replied in a lowered voice, "Of course not. Why would I deny it when there was a pub full of witnesses?" His voice was much quieter now as he didn't want Sarah to hear.

The inspector continued, "But you deny that it was you who threw the brick at his window last night?"

"Of course, I do. That would be too obvious, wouldn't it? And anyway, if it was last night, I was at work. I work nights, you see. Last night was my last for this shift pattern, and now I'm trying to enjoy a rare weekend off work." Sarcasm rippled through his words.

The inspector didn't want to antagonise him further, but he still had questions. "May I ask what your work hours are, please? You understand that I will need to verify your information."

"I start at 10 pm and knock off at 6 am. Now, can we get these prints done?" said Mike, keen to get on.

The inspector responded calmly to Mike's aggressive tone. "We can do that shortly. My DC has the equipment. How much time do you have Mr Tennant?"

Mike glanced at his watch again and began to fidget anxiously. "I can spare you ten minutes," he said, as he began to calm down. "Then I'll need to go. I have to get to the chemist before it closes."

"Nothing serious, I hope?" the inspector asked.

"Look, you obviously overheard us arguing just now." Mike looked at the inspector with a mix of anxiety and desperation, before asking, "If I tell you something, can you promise it won't go any further?"

The inspector picked up the teapot and said, "I'll be Mum, shall I?" and, pouring as he spoke, he continued, "Mr Tennant, discretion is my middle name, as long as it's not illegal."

Mike lowered his voice further and spoke in a hushed tone. "You noticed Sarah's ankle is in a cast, right?"

The inspector nodded and Mike continued, "Well, the reason for her broken ankle is that she secretly stopped taking her medication."

Exhausted from a lack of sleep and his defences lowered, his demeanour underwent a noticeable shift. He pulled out a chair from the kitchen table and invited the inspector to sit down. "Please, have a seat, Inspector. I'll tell you everything you need to know, but you have to promise to keep it between us."

The inspector replied, "Mr Tennant, I do a thorough job and will check anything that I deem important. However, I can assure you, I do not idly gossip about personal matters."

In a deadly serious tone, Mike continued, "What I am about to tell you is highly confidential and it's crucial it remains that way. I'm only telling you because you're likely to come across it when you make your checks. Can I trust you? Do I have your word, Inspector?"

The inspector realised the gravity of Mike's tone and replied, "I repeat, we don't idly gossip. I can guarantee you that any information you provide will only be shared with those who need to know."

Mike hesitated before he continued. "Well, I'm sure some people in this village think I'm a real misery because I lead a very private life. But Sarah is my life; she always has been. She just needs a little extra care than your average woman. It's not her fault, you know, as she had a tough start in life. And it's no one else's business."

He paused and took a large gulp of his tea, as he checked his watch again. "Don't let me miss that chemist, will you?" He paused and wondered if he should confide in the inspector or whether it would be better to take a trip to the police station after all.

The inspector waited patiently for him to speak.

"Look, what rank did you say you were? Because you really can't tell anyone. I ought to make a phone call and check with someone else first or come down to the station later," Mike said, before clamming up.

"Ring whoever you need to, Mr Tennant. I'm in no rush."

Mike checked his watch again. "Yes, but I am. Are you absolutely sure it will go no further?"

"Over the years, Sir, there's not a lot I haven't seen. If it warrants secrecy, you have my word."

Mike felt sufficiently reassured, took a deep breath, and began. "Look, Sarah had been through a lot by the time she arrived in the village. It took years for me to get to the truth but, when I did, I was shocked. She and her mother moved here to live in a safe place, somewhere where her father could never find them. They changed their names, identities and lifestyle. Her father went to prison for abusing them both but, worse still, he had brutally harmed her younger sister, so badly that she needed lifelong medical and personal care."

Mike paused for a second as he put his head in his hands, fully anticipating the inspector to say something but he didn't. He wasn't even making notes.

Mike continued with his explanation, "Sarah seemed to cope well. As she grew up, though, her mental health suffered, and she's been on one sort of pill or another to keep her stable ever since. It was only when her mother passed away, after a brief illness, swiftly followed by her sister, that she began to struggle. I was just glad to be around to help her through it all and, one thing led to another and eventually, we got married."

The inspector gestured for him to carry on.

"That was some ten years ago now and, over the years, I've learnt from experience that as long as Sarah keeps up with her meds, she's fine. It's just that, sometimes, after a decent run of being normal, no let me change that; 'normal' isn't the right word. After being well, she convinces herself she's fine and doesn't need her pills. That's when things go wrong, which usually ends up with her being a little worse for wear. Inspector, she's always blamed herself for not being able to look after her mum and sister."

The inspector replied compassionately, "That's a big secret you have there, Mr Tennant, and very admirable of you to keep it so well. Thank you for sharing that with me. Am I right that you don't have children?"

"Yes, you are, and we're not likely to. Sarah has always said she doesn't want the responsibility and, after all that she's been through, I can understand why. To be a dad would be great but choosing between Sarah with no kids, or someone else with kids, then there's no competition. I knew what my future would be like when I asked her to marry me."

The inspector nodded understandingly, and tried to keep him on track by asking, "Can you enlighten me then, please, what happens when Sarah feels she no longer needs her medication?"

"She does it secretively but I can always tell, eventually. Her behaviour becomes exaggerated and extreme, and she normally ends up with an injury."

Suddenly, his tone of voice changed and he started to get angry. "I know what people say, those bloody nosey village folk. They all talk behind my back and jump to the obvious, but wrong, conclusion. They assume I'm some sort of woman-beater and that I slap her around. If only they knew the truth. But it's like this, Inspector. I decided years ago that it was no one else's business. I'm happy to stay out of other people's lives and I don't want anyone meddling in ours. We trust the medical team we see from time to time, but that's it. Oh yes, we also have an update with the Police Protection Team every few years. You can check that. I'm sure you will. But, other than that, we're pretty self-sufficient and Sarah never speaks of her past."

The inspector silently drank his tea. He didn't want to interrupt Mike's flow, so he listened and encouraged him to continue.

"I've heard them, you know, when we pass someone in the street, or the pub, whispering behind my back. 'Poor Sarah, look what he's done to her this time,' they say. I never correct them though. I wouldn't want Sarah to be caught up in any confrontation. Understand this, I can't be clearer regarding Sarah. I don't care what others think of me, as long as she's okay. For better or for worse, in sickness and in health, as the vows say. I made a promise. I'm sure as hell going to stick to it."

"That's very admirable, Mr Tennant. I imagine it must be challenging for you. If you don't mind my asking, how is Sarah doing today?"

"I thought you might ask. She's struggling with mood swings. She seemed fine earlier but, after lunch, she turned and became argumentative. During her darkest moments, she says heart-breaking things; wishing she had died instead of her sister. I guess you're wondering about her ankle."

Inspector Southerby nodded, "I would be lying if I didn't, Sir."

"Well, a few weeks ago, she was having a particularly troubled time and wanted to end it all, so she threw herself down the stairs. Fortunately, she only had a broken ankle and a few bruises. That's why I have to make sure that she takes her medication. It's tough sometimes, but I do my best." He let out a sigh, as he looked towards the bin containing the broken glass.

The inspector consoled him. "I'm sure you do, Mr Tennant. It can't be easy looking out for her all the time, especially working shifts."

"You're not wrong. The more I try to help, the more she insists on doing everything herself. Eventually, I gave in and agreed that she could make her own way to work. I secretly kept a watchful eye from a distance, in case she needed help. When I saw her accepting help from a stranger, I have to admit that I was not best pleased."

Meanwhile, Sarah and Hicks had been chatting in the living room. "I don't know where they've gone for that tea. China maybe. I'll check," said Sarah, as she reached for her crutches.

Hicks jumped up. "No, let me, please." But Sarah was having none of it and snapped back, "No, sit down, I've got this!"

Hicks immediately sat down, as if she had been reprimanded by a teacher. Sarah hobbled to the kitchen, pausing for just a moment at the door to rearrange her crutches, and was just in time to overhear the inspector say, "Ah, I see, so that's how you know that she accepted help?"

Sarah pushed hard on the kitchen door with one of her crutches, and the door swung open, hitting the wall. "I heard that," she shouted. "I can't believe you've been snooping on me." Furious, she returned to her armchair, slumping into it. "No wonder you don't believe me when I say I can manage on my own."

Mike jumped up and followed her, saying, "Well, what do you expect? You'll accept help from a stranger, but not from your husband."

The inspector knew he needed to defuse the situation if he was going to make any progress with his enquiries. Attempting to change the subject, he said, "I'm sure your husband only had good intentions. Now, how about those fingerprints?"

Turning to Mike, he continued, "Thank you for being so understanding, Mr Tennant. It's just a procedure and, as I mentioned, it will help to eliminate you from our enquiries. Hicks, could you please get the kit?" Turning back to Sarah, he said, "We'll take your husband's fingerprints as soon as possible, and then we can leave you in peace."

Hicks rushed to the car and quickly returned to take Mike's fingerprints while the inspector sat with Sarah.

"You know, Mrs Tennant, my DC is right. You do have a lovely place here. I wish my house was as nice as this, but I'm never there to sort it out."

"All done," announced Hicks, as she packed away the kit and the inspector stood up to leave. "We'll be leaving now. We don't want to take any more of your time," he said as they made their way towards the front door.

Mike was curious to know and asked, just as they were about to leave, "Inspector, you never said, but what time was the window smashed?"

The inspector turned round, calmly stating, "No, I didn't, did I? It was around 9:45 pm. Thanks for your time, and I hope we won't need to bother you again."

After closing the front door, Mike turned to Sarah, who met him with an angry expression, and silence.

"I need to get to the chemist before they close. If I wait any longer, I'll have to go all the way into town." Leaning forward, Mike attempted to give Sarah a quick kiss on the cheek, but she pushed him away. "Don't be upset, please. I'll be back as soon as I can, and we can talk then." Grabbing his truck keys, he rushed out of the house.

Sixteen

Saturday mid afternoon

"Well, that was fun, wasn't it?" announced Inspector Southerby, smiling as he stepped into the car. "Now Hicks, take us back to headquarters, please."

As they pulled away, he dragged a specimen bag from one of his jacket pockets and, with great care, a saucer from the other. Carefully placing the saucer in the bag, he said, "When we get back, we can gather our thoughts and share our discoveries."

"Is Sarah's saucer part of your discoveries as well, Sir? I saw you take that. You're lucky no one else did," replied Hicks, as she drove out of the village.

"Yes, I suppose it is. I just need to double-check something and need to do my homework. Come on, Hicks, you're not driving Miss Daisy. You'll need to step on it if you want to interview the landlady later."

Back at the police station, Inspector Southerby was full of enthusiasm and orders. He passed the bagged saucer to Hicks.

"Here, get this off to Forensics urgently for fingerprints, and make sure you tell them I want full details, whatever they find. Be clear though, FULL DETAILS."

His orders kept coming. "On your way back, can you get me a coffee?"

Hanging his jacket on the back of his chair, he walked over to the incident boards, shouting out, "Where have all the marker pens disappeared to?" He didn't get a response from Hicks, who was already halfway down the corridor on her way to the forensics department. Alone in the incident room, he pulled up a chair and began examining the boards.

Hicks soon returned, drinks in her hand and marker pens in her pocket. "Forensics said we would get the results as soon as they have them, Sir." She passed the inspector his drink and reached into her pocket to pull out several marker pens. Smiling, she continued, "I heard you shouting for these halfway down the corridor. Any preference on colour?" She spread them out like a pack of cards.

The inspector raised his eyebrows at her and took a sip of his coffee. Quickly pulling the cup away and making a face, he complained loudly, "This isn't coffee! What are you trying to do? Poison me?"

Laughing she replied, "Okay, okay. Calm down Sir. It's only hot chocolate. It's not going to kill you. Sorry, that's mine. Here, let's swap," she said, passing him the right drink.

"Not so fast there, young Hicks. If it's all the same to you, now I know what it is, I think I'll keep it," he said, grinning. "I'm quite partial to a hot chocolate occasionally, and I'll have a red and a black pen, please."

Keeping the coffee, she pulled up a chair next to him. "I see you're looking at the incident boards, Sir. Any ideas?"

"Which case do you want to discuss first? The brick through the window or the more exciting murder case?"

"I didn't realise I had a choice," she replied, smiling. "Although your chat with Mike Tennant fascinates me. You were in the kitchen for ages. What did you discover there, Sir?"

"Don't judge a book by its cover is what I'll say about that one," the inspector cautioned. "You're right to be fascinated though, as it's even more interesting than you might imagine. Let's start by writing up what we can about Mike Tennant. There must be a spare incident board in here somewhere. Have you seen one anywhere?" He stood up and began scanning the room. "Ah ha, no worries, there's one hiding behind the door."

Hicks looked up and could see the chief super intendant coming down the corridor towards them. Meanwhile, the inspector was about to push the heavy oak-panelled door closed to retrieve the incident board. She tried to stop him by calling out, "Look out, we're about to have a …"

But it was too late. The breeze caught the door, slamming it with considerable force in the chief super intendant's face. Unaware of this, and pleased with himself for retrieving the board, the inspector said, "Blimey, the wind caught that quickly, didn't it? Anyway, what were you saying, Hicks."

"I was trying to tell you that we were about to have a visitor."

Just then, the door opened and the chief super intendant stood in its deep archway. Straightening his jacket and clearing his throat, he said in a slow, serious voice, "Good afternoon. Working late today, aren't you, Inspector? Don't you usually push off at lunchtime on

Saturdays?" Turning to Hicks, he continued, "You know there's no money in the budget for overtime this month, don't you? I do hope Southerby isn't keeping you here under false pretences."

"Oh, that's not a problem. We're just chatting through our findings before we go, aren't we, Sir?"

Inspector Southerby smiled at Hicks before declaring, "I would never keep anyone here who didn't want to be here, Chief Super Intendant. But as long as you're here, why don't you join us, and we can bring you up to date on this murder case. Come and have a seat." He walked across the office and patted one of the chairs, saying, "Come on over, don't be shy."

The chief declined, preferring to remain in the doorway.

"Okay then. Anyway, Sir, we have uniform lined up for further interviews on Monday morning at the train station, as well as tracing what small family the victim had. He doesn't seem to have any immediate family locally, nor any friends, as he's not lived here long. Think we might have to look further afield on this one, Sir. So, my plan is this …"

The chief interrupted firmly. "No need to give me all the details, Southerby. I have pressing matters elsewhere. Just keep me informed of any significant developments. Don't forget, we want to secure the arrest of whoever did this as swiftly as possible. We can't have a murderer on the loose, can we?"

"Don't you worry, Chief, we'll catch the culprit. You go off and enjoy your weekend."

The chief turned to leave, thanking him as he went, not sure if the inspector was being sarcastic or not.

"You push your luck with the chief, don't you? Did you realise you practically slammed the door in his face?" asked Hicks.

"Really! Accidental that, purely accidental. I couldn't have timed it better if I'd tried," he said, laughing. "Now then, back to the matter at hand. To be honest, I think we've come to a bit of a dead end with our murder victim, excuse the pun. All apart from one comment you made earlier that's been playing on my mind."

"Oh, damn," cursed Hicks, interrupting his thoughts. "I didn't realise the time. Look, I should have said earlier, I've got plans for this afternoon. But I can still interview the landlady at the pub afterwards. Is it okay if I push off?" She glanced at her watch, hopefully.

"I suppose I can't say no. We're already on unpaid extra time, but I haven't told you about Mike Tennant..." He stopped abruptly, remembering that before he could discuss the Tennant's secret, he had to wait for the forensics report to come back. That would verify Sarah's new identity.

"Okay, you get off and I'll get the paperwork up to date."

"Thanks, Sir. I'll be in touch if there's anything new to tell you, once I've spoken to the landlady."

She dragged her handbag out of her desk drawer and headed for the door. As she left, the inspector strode towards the collection of incident boards, armed with the collection of new marker pens. He was determined to write up their findings before stopping for the day and hoped that inspiration would strike in the process.

Hicks didn't waste any time and was already on her way to town. She had been promising herself some retail therapy for weeks and wasn't going to let another weekend pass without it. Filled with determination, she swiftly parked her car and made her way towards the shops. Despite thoroughly exploring every store, nothing caught her eye, and the only thing she gained was a pair of sore feet.

As she checked her watch, her stomach growled and reminded her that it was almost teatime. Time must have slipped away and the shops were starting to close. Disappointed with her timekeeping, and running late for her meeting with the landlady, she hurried back to her car, briefly wishing she could use her blue light. Regardless, she made good time getting back to the village and managed to park her car near the pub.

She approached the side door of the pub, as instructed and knocked, but no one answered. Aware how late in the day it was, she concluded that the landlady had probably returned to the bar for her evening shift.

She pondered her options. If she walked into the pub, the landlady might not appreciate having a police officer there again. She stepped back from the door, wondering what Inspector Southerby would do in this situation.

Suddenly, a man came rushing around the corner, so fast that he bumped into her and knocked her to the ground. Before she could react, she heard a familiar voice, offering help.

"I'm sorry. Here, take my hand. I hope you're okay." She looked up and saw Mike Tennant. Accepting his help, she gushed out, with a hint of embarrassment, "It was my fault, sorry. I didn't see you coming. I'm fine, really. Just a little bruised pride."

As she brushed down her clothes, Mike replied, "Well, maybe it was mine but I'll let you take the blame. I don't want to be done for assaulting a police officer, do I?"

Smiling at her, he continued, "As long as you're not hurt." He paused for a moment and his expression quickly changed to one of concern. "Sorry, I can't stop. I've got to find Sarah."

Then, scanning the surrounding area to see if anyone was within earshot, he continued to speak in a lowered voice. "After your earlier visit, the village chemist was closed, so I had to go to town to get Sarah's prescription. When I got back, she wasn't there. I thought maybe she'd just gone for a short walk, so I waited. I tried her mobile but no answer, so I've been out searching the village but I can't find her anywhere. Look, I'm probably overreacting but, if you see her, could you bring her home, please? Anyway, I'm glad you're not hurt. I'll be seeing you."

He quickly hurried away.

Hicks concluded that it was probably best to skip the pub and reschedule in the morning. Instead, she decided to have a quick look around for Sarah, convinced she couldn't have gone far on her crutches. After completing several circuits of the village with no sighting and, as Mike hadn't reported anything, she assumed all was well. With nothing arranged for the rest of the day, but curious to see the inspector's notes, she returned to the station, picking up fish and chips on the way.

Seventeen

Saturday late afternoon

Swinging open the heavy front door, Howard looked at the temporary repair to the window.

"It's an eyesore, isn't it? Never mind, let's find this dog and take him for a run." Raising his voice, he called out, "Charlie, where are you?"

Walking into the kitchen, Seraphina and Howard saw Charlie curled up in his bed. His ears were down and he looked guilty but was wagging his tail. "Some guard dog you are. You don't even get out of your bed to greet us, let alone bark!" joked Howard.

"You talk to that dog like he understands every word you say," said Seraphina, grabbing the dog lead from the hook on the kitchen wall. She called out, "Here, catch!" and threw the lead over to Howard, who nonchalantly stretched out his arm and beamed as he caught it.

"Okay, I'll let you have that one. I suppose you look cool on the rare occasions you do catch it," Seraphina smiled. "Right then, let's burn some lunch off and walk Charlie over to the common. Come on, get your boots on, and let's go before the day disappears."

Howard was feeling grateful for how vibrant and full of life Seraphina was today. He couldn't help thinking that last night was a significant moment for her, a turning point perhaps. Determined not to dampen her spirits, he hastily put on his walking boots and slipped a tennis ball into his pocket before putting Charlie's leash on him. After a quick check for his keys, he opened the front door, allowing Seraphina to lead the way. They chatted as they walked, and Charlie tugged at the lead.

"You spoke to quite a variety of people at the pub after lunch. Did you enjoy yourself?" asked Howard.

"Yes, I did, although I'm no closer to finding out who broke our window! Call me crazy or naïve, but I was sure the pub was the heart of the village. I thought I'd be able to rock up, speak to a few people, and find out who was responsible. No one seemed to know anything, or they were unwilling to speak up. Don't get me wrong. It was pleasant, and lunch was lovely, just not what I'd imagined. Do you think they knew something but kept it to themselves?"

"I don't know, Darling, but I do know that we should let the police sort it out. It could be anyone in the village. Look, let's forget about it for a while and enjoy the rest of today." He tried to change the subject, by saying, "Ah, look at Charlie. He's calmed down and he's walking well on his lead now. At last, he must be learning. As it's such a lovely day, let's take the long way round to the common. We would never do this on a Saturday evening at our old place, would we?"

"Yes, I must admit it is nice, but then we never had a dog before," she replied, turning to Howard, raising her eyebrows and grinning.

He was quick to respond. "Only because you wouldn't let me!" he said, pretending to be angry. He gently nudged her with his elbow, just as they rounded a corner.

Seraphina stumbled and would have fallen over had it not been for Ziggy and Chris walking in the opposite direction. As she began to fall, Ziggy, as quick as lightning, leapt forward and caught her with both arms.

In his usual bold and amateur-dramatic manner, he held her up like an offering to Howard and announced, "Your wife, I believe." He laughed loudly, as he gently placed her back on the ground, feet first.

"Hey guys, I hope you don't think I habitually push her around. We were only messing about but thanks for catching her fall, Ziggy, literally," said Howard. As Seraphina straightened her clothes, she reflected on how Ziggy had caught her so effortlessly.

Howard continued, "How are you two today then?"

"We are most excellent, aren't we, Chris?" replied Ziggy.

Chris agreed. "Yes, we are. Actually, we were just off to the pub for a quick pint, then we had plans to visit your house later."

Seraphina jumped into the conversation, excited. "Really? I bet you want to see what we've done with the place, don't you?"

Ziggy smiled at them. "That would be very nice as well, but we have something we want to talk to you about. I guess one might call it a proposition."

"Oh," said Howard, cautiously, "I don't know if that sounds exciting or ominous."

"Well, hopefully, it will be exciting," added Chris.

Howard paused for a second, before replying, "Look, we're going to be a little while yet, walking this *hound of hell*." They all looked at Charlie, who was already on his back, with Ziggy rubbing his tummy! "Why don't you

179

come round about 6 pm and join us for a bite to eat? We were talking earlier about trying that new Chinese takeaway that's just opened on the high street. What do you think?"

"That's a great idea," agreed Seraphina, excited at the thought of having guests.

Ziggy accepted, saying, "OK, let's do that then."

"Any allergies, gentlemen?" asked Seraphina, looking at both of them but struggling to keep her eyes off Ziggy.

"No, we're all good with anything. Do you have a takeaway menu?" asked Chris.

"I don't think we have," replied Seraphina.

"Right then," bellowed Ziggy in his usual manner. "Here's the plan. We'll pick one up on our way round and we can order when we get to yours. Sound good? Of course, it does. That's decided then. We'll see you later. Now then, Chris, onwards. Take me to the pub!"

They went on their way and Seraphina called out, "See you later. I'm so intrigued, I can hardly wait."

It wasn't long before they were on the common, playing a game of fetch with Charlie, when a black Labrador came running up to them, barking loudly. Convinced he recognised the Labrador, Howard looked around for the owner, as they tried to calm the two dogs.

"I'm coming," shouted someone in the distance. Howard turned to the direction of the voice and saw Pauline running as fast as she could towards them, whilst Seraphina tried to calm the Labrador. Eventually joining them, but out of breath, she apologised. "I'm so sorry. When he saw Charlie, he ran to join him as quickly as he could. I don't know why he barks so much."

When she reached into her pocket she immediately had both dogs' full attention and their silence. One treat each and they were off, playing together like a couple of puppies and running around all over the common.

"How nice to see you Pauline," said Howard. "How's your hand now?"

Pauline held out her hand and replied, "Looks like my butterfly stitches and Germolene are doing the trick."

Seraphina leaned forward to look more closely at her hand, saying, "Oh, my god. That looks really sore. You must have cut it on something sharp. How did you do it?"

Howard interrupted by saying, "Don't you remember me telling you how I helped Pauline take in her delivery the other morning because of it?"

Seraphina looked at him blankly. "Well, no actually, I don't. I remember you going on about visiting the corner shop, but you said nothing about Pauline and her hand." She turned to Pauline and said, "I hope your tetanus is up to date. Are you sure you shouldn't have gone to A&E with that?"

Pauline laughed, saying, "Funny, that's exactly what Howard said I should've done. But I'm fine, really, thanks." She called out, "Come on, Buster, time to go. It's been nice seeing you both and letting the dogs play together. See you again soon, I hope."

Buster came to Pauline's call this time and, after she put his lead on, they left.

Seraphina and Howard played fetch with Charlie a while longer before heading home themselves. As they walked, Seraphina replayed the events of the last few days through her mind before bombarding Howard with a string of questions. "Pauline and her hand; was it the same morning that poor man at the train station got stabbed, Howard? Didn't you say he died in her arms? What time did he get stabbed? What time did you see her? Was it a knife she cut herself with?" Her mind was racing but, this time, Howard knew exactly what she was thinking.

"Now then, please stop playing the detective with that vivid imagination of yours. You always do this, and normally put two and two together and inevitably end up with twenty-two! No, it wasn't Pauline. I was with her when the guy at the station got stabbed. No, hold on, was I?" He paused for a moment. "Actually, I couldn't have been because she was at the station. It must have been the day before. Oh, I don't flipping know. One day blends into the next at the moment. The sooner I get a job, the better I suppose. At least I'd know what day of the week it was," he said, laughing.

She looked at him and raised one eyebrow, a trick she'd always been able to do, and smiled, saying, "Come on you. I promise not to play detective if you promise to make up your mind about what you want to do with your life."

Once home, Seraphina spent ages speculating about Chris and Ziggy's proposition. She suggested optimistically, "What if Chris is thinking of retiring and is going to offer me the business, or what about a partnership?" She quickly followed in the next breath with, "Oh no, what if it's not good news? What if they're coming to let me down gently and tell me that Chris doesn't need me anymore, and he's bringing Ziggy along for support?"

She was driving herself crazy. Howard interrupted her line of thought before she got too carried away.

"Don't be so ridiculous. You heard them. They said it was all good, whatever 'all good' is. We'll find out very soon, so speculating will get you nowhere. Why don't you put the kettle on and I'll get the table ready."

EIGHTEEN

Saturday early evening

The doorbell chimed precisely at 6 pm.

"I bet that's Ziggy and Chris. What punctuality!" said Seraphina. "Can you get it, please? I'm busy sorting glasses for the table, thanks."

"I'm on it," called Howard, as he approached the door. "Hold your horses. I'm coming as fast as I can."

As he swung the door open, he found Ziggy and Chris standing there, arms full of bags and giggling. In unison, they declared their arrival, and, in their eagerness to enter, both attempted to cross the threshold simultaneously, resulting in a comical situation akin to a 'Laurel and Hardy' scene. Howard stood aside, amused and unable to contain his laughter as he beckoned Seraphina and joked, "I've discovered two strange individuals on the doorstep and I'm letting them in."

Having never set foot in the house before, Ziggy confidently declared, "I know the way, Chris, follow me."

They walked through to the kitchen and carelessly dumped their bags on the new marble-top kitchen island with a loud thud. Seraphina whirled around abruptly and focused on the worktop. Ziggy noticed her gaze and jokingly remarked, "I see you checking it out. Don't worry.

If I've broken your worktop, Seraphina, I'll buy you a new one." He flashed the widest tipsy smile he could muster.

Pointing at the bags, Chris announced, "Look, we brought food. Old boozer, Ziggy here, made us drink more than just one pint. So, on our way here, we stopped by the Chinese and grabbed their set menu for four, and some wine and beer. I hope that's okay." He was desperately attempting to appear more sober than he was.

Howard replied, "That sounds great to me. No need to stand on ceremony here. Come and sit down at the table while we get this ready." As he opened the first bag, he turned to Seraphina and remarked, "Look, Darling, they've used tinfoil trays, so they won't melt if we use a couple of those tealight food-warmer things." Seraphina nodded, understanding precisely what he meant, promptly found them, and placed them on the table.

Ziggy chipped in, "Can I help?" and Chris followed suit, "And me." Although Seraphina would typically take the lead in arranging the food, time was of the essence and Chris and Ziggy had already started taking various dishes and piling them up on the warming trays. Howard deftly sorted drinks for everyone, even adding a couple of chilled water bottles to the table, just in case. Soon, they were all relishing their Chinese dinner.

"That's much better. I enjoyed that. I was just beginning to feel a teensy-weensy bit tipsy," announced Ziggy, as he carefully placed his knife and fork together on his plate.

As everyone laughed out loud, Howard said, "You don't say. If only you could have seen the two of you trying to cross the threshold earlier. It was incredibly amusing."

Chris, who was gradually sobering up, began, "Well, I'm blaming that on Ziggy. He does this every time and you'd think I'd know better by now. It's that infamous 'just one pint' suggestion that lures me out of the house and then, once we're at the pub, it quickly turns into two or more. Time whizzed by, then Ziggy started talking about food and, well, here we are." He beamed as he looked at Ziggy and squeezed his hand. Howard noticed and looked at Seraphina.

Seraphina glanced at Chris and Ziggy, and a sudden realisation of her foolishness struck her. In an instant, she recalled all the times she had admired Chris's impeccable fashion sense, his flawlessly manicured beard, and his charm; how she considered him a classy, yet cool guy, who was easy to talk to and so very understanding, especially when she was upset in the office. Her thoughts turned to Ziggy and she felt like a complete idiot. It was painfully obvious now that she had been foolishly swooning over a man who would never reciprocate her feelings. She berated herself for being so easily flattered by kind words from anyone other than Howard.

"You all right there, Seraphina? You look like you've seen a ghost!" said Ziggy, noticing how she had drifted away from the conversation.

All eyes focused on her. She felt very foolish and wanted to move on quickly. Taking a breath and clearing her throat, she replied, "Oh, I'm fine, thanks. Just trying to decide if I should open another bottle or make some coffee."

Chris announced, "Let's not top up our glasses just yet. Now we've both sobered up a little, it's probably an opportune time to come clean about the reason for our visit." He looked at Ziggy and raised his eyebrows in an encouraging manner. "The floor is yours now, Mate."

"Okay, well, I think you both know by now that I'm some kind of arty-farty person," said Ziggy. Howard nodded, and Seraphina giggled at his description.

"Shall I put that as your occupation on your next tax return?"

"Yes, why not? I'd love to see what HMRC would have to say about that."

Chris smacked his forehead with the palm of his hand, saying, "See what I have to deal with, guys!"

Ziggy joked, "Excuse me, everyone. All eyes on me please, this is where it's at. Thanks, Chris, I'll continue now, if I may."

Putting his elbows on the table and leaning into Seraphina and Howard, he continued, "Well, look, my work can range from being a small piece of art that sits on a sideboard in someone's house to, let's say, a large piece in someone's garden, or bigger."

Seraphina interrupted. "Or a massive one, with lots of horses like the one …"

"Yes, okay, so you have seen my work. Do you like it? No, don't answer that. That's not what we're here for."

"We love it," said Howard. "Especially the large pieces. They would make magnificent pictures, you know. I've seen them on the internet. I could imagine them blown up on enormous posters." Realising that he was taking the conversation in a different direction, he stopped himself, saying, "Oh, sorry, I digress. You carry on and don't let us interrupt again."

"Okay, well, here's the thing. I've been at this game for a long time now and often have to work away when a large piece is being set up. I need someone back at headquarters to take care of the planning and project management. Not all my work is based outdoors and, for those pieces, I'd like to open a gallery. But that's a great idea you have there, Howard. Posters of my larger pieces would be good."

After taking the last sip from his glass, he paused, as if he was savouring the taste before he continued. "Guys, there's a place on the high street that I've had my eye on for years. It has a beautiful shop front, with large windows and a fabulous workshop at the back, bathed in wonderful natural light. Chris and I have been discussing it, and the timing seems perfect."

He turned to Howard and continued, "Chris mentioned how you managed the entire renovation of this Grade 2 listed property by yourself. It must have been quite a challenge. That's why, when we were looking for a suitable manager, you were the obvious choice."

Howard took a large gulp from his glass, giving himself time to compose his thoughts. "I apologise, but I just want to be certain. Are you saying that you want me to manage the new place?" He turned to Ziggy and Chris, who beamed at him and nodded in agreement.

"I'm completely taken aback! I thought you were going to tell us that Chris was joining you and you were shutting down the accountancy business."

Seraphina chipped in hastily, "I was thinking the same."

Howard's expression suddenly turned serious.

"What's the matter, Howard?" asked Chris, who had been watching his response closely while Ziggy was talking.

Howard hesitated, glancing nervously around the table. He realised that the occasion called for honesty. "Well, if I can be frank with you all, I know I've tested Seraphina's patience long enough about getting a job. But there's a good reason." He turned in his chair and looked directly at her. "Honestly, Seraphina, there is. I guess now would be the right time to come clean."

"Christ, Howard, you've got me worried now!" said Seraphina, immediately echoed by Chris and Ziggy.

He quickly looked around the table and could see the anxious expressions on all their faces. He replied, "Oh, there's no need to worry. Everything's fine." He was uncertain how they would react, but he realised it was the perfect moment to confess.

Taking a deep breath, he continued. "Well, I've been working on something I've wanted to do for years, and I'm very close to finishing it. Seraphina, you know all those times you thought I was wasting time surfing the internet, or writing in my diary?" She silently acknowledged this with a quick nod. Howard was on a roll and continued, "Well, a lot of that time, I've been writing. I guess you could call it a novel." He followed up quickly, saying, "And I've almost finished it."

"Wow, I'm impressed. I knew we had a creative bond, Howard; I could sense it," said Ziggy. "Tell me, tell us all. What's it about?" Ziggy was genuinely intrigued and excited for him.

"It's based, as you might expect, in the world of investments and finance. It's full of deception, insider-dealing, and double-crossing. It's strange though, I feel like I've been living a life of deceit whilst writing it. You see guys, I've been hiding it from Seraphina."

He turned and looked at her. "I'm sorry for all the stress I've put you through. I've let you think I've been job-hunting when I haven't. I didn't want to say anything because, well, for all I know, it might be rubbish."

"Well, I certainly didn't see that one coming. I suppose you won't be interested in our offer anymore then, will you?" asked Chris.

Before Howard could reply, Seraphina spoke up, reminding him, "Howard, you know how I was saying you should decide what you want to do with your life? Well, maybe this is decision time. What is it you truly want to do?"

Chris sensed he needed some time to think and suggested, "Howard, we didn't expect you to give us an answer right away. How about this? You give us a copy of what you've written so far, and we can give you some constructive feedback. Meanwhile, you can take some time to consider our offer. Let's meet back in a few days for a book review, perhaps over an Indian, and we can take it from there. What do you say? There's no pressure at all."

"That's a great idea but, remember, our offer will be rubbish money and long hours!" Ziggy said laughing.

"Oh, Ziggy, you're certainly selling it to me," chuckled Howard. "To be honest, I'm slightly nervous about anyone reading it, but okay, I'll put some paper in the printer and set it running in a minute."

Ziggy asked, "What's it called?"

"Oh, I haven't decided yet. Maybe the two of you could give me some suggestions?"

Seraphina cleared her throat sarcastically loudly. "Excuse me, but this is news to me as well. When do I get to read it?"

"Oh, sorry Seraphina. Yes, I'll run you off a copy as well. Give me a minute. I'll just run down to the study and set the printer going."

He was there and back in no time. Meanwhile, Ziggy couldn't contain his excitement and exclaimed, "I can already imagine it! Visitors to my gallery will not only see my art but also get to meet a famous author. Of course, until that day arrives, you might just make enough to pay for the broken window we noticed on our way in. Oh, but obviously, only if you're interested in our offer. Seriously, no pressure, but wouldn't that be wonderful?"

Chris quickly interjected, "Ziggy, let's change the subject and allow Howard and Seraphina to think about it in their own time. Sorry guys, he is so impulsive."

Ziggy defended himself. "I prefer to think of myself as spontaneous. Oh, and flamboyant, and creative, with a sensitive nature and …"

Chris interrupted and teased him. "Don't forget modest, will you? You're such a theatrical diva."

"Anyway," Ziggy continued, "before I was so rudely interrupted, tell me, how did your window get broken? I bet you weren't happy. They're quite old, aren't they?"

Seraphina replied, "Ah, I wondered if you'd notice. It's all been going on here. We had the police out last night and everything! First, though, does anyone want a coffee? I'm going to have one, and then we'll tell you all about it." She jumped up and grabbed the rotating coffee pod dispenser. Placing it in the middle of the table and giving it a spin, she said, "There you go, guys. You choose your coffee pod, and I'll do the rest."

"Excuse my wife, but she loves these kitchen-gadget thingies. I'm more of a traditionalist myself. If I had my way, I'd have an old-fashioned coffee grinder plus one of those machines that filter the hot water through the ground coffee and you can steam the milk; like you see in proper coffee shops." He smiled at Seraphina, knowing she would protest.

"Are you reminiscing about your city days, Howard darling? Come on boys, make up your minds about what flavour of coffee you want. I can't wait to tell you about our window."

She hovered at the table impatiently as they each chose a pod and passed it to her. As she made the coffee, she began to explain.

"So, yesterday, I came home as usual after leaving work. We had a lovely evening, planning our trip to Kew Gardens, when we heard a bang and smashing of glass. Some idiot had only gone and thrown a bloody great brick through our window!"

Chris gasped in disbelief, "No way! You're kidding?"

"Way!" said Howard quickly and burst out laughing. Seraphina glared at him, surprised at his comment.

"Sorry, I shouldn't be so flippant. I just couldn't resist. I heard someone say that on TV just the other night. You carry on, Sweetheart," he said, as he smiled at her.

"Yes, I will, if you can hold back on interrupting me. Anyway, Chris, no, I'm not kidding and there's more! Guess what? Just like in the films, it had a message wrapped around it!"

Intrigued, Ziggy asked, "Blimey! What did the note say?"

"Now let me get this right. It said, 'You're not welcome here. Leave now or suffer the consequences,' and it was in cut-out letters from a newspaper, just like you see on TV, so we rang the police. They turned up really quickly and took all the details. There were two of them, and they seemed genuinely kind. I got on well with DC Hicks; she was lovely. Anyway, they're looking into it."

Howard added, "As you can see, we didn't get to Kew Gardens as planned. Instead, Seraphina has been trying to play detective all day. She's dragged me all over the village and insisted we go to the pub for lunch, just so she could interrogate the locals. We even crossed paths with the police and you ended up with a warning, didn't you, Sweetheart?"

"No, I didn't!" she protested, as she handed round the coffees.

Howard grinned. "I see, so when the inspector said, 'Leave the policing to us', what do you think he meant by that?"

"Okay, okay, so I was snooping around a bit, but can you blame me? What kind of idiot goes around smashing windows? And, to be honest, the message was a little alarming. If we were of a weaker disposition, we would be terrified. We're not though, are we, Howard?"

He looked at her and was about to recall the delicate state she was in the previous night. She looked back at him and, knowing exactly what he was thinking, continued, "Okay. If I'm absolutely honest, I was a little rattled at first. But, today, I'm not. I'm over it and I'm convinced it's that bloke who had a go at Howard in the pub the other night. I told the police all about it, and I'm sure they will sort him out and let us know when they catch up with him." Her mind was racing as she continued, "They might even come and interview you two as well. They definitely wanted to talk to the landlady when we were there, didn't they, Howard?"

"Hold on there. So you're saying your broken window wasn't an accident? This is terrible!" declared Chris.

Ziggy nodded in agreement. "Yes, this is awful. How on earth did you get any sleep last night? How can you stop here while the police are figuring out what's happened and with a broken window?"

"Yes, come and stop at ours. Just until the police finish their enquiries, and the window is fixed," offered Chris.

Seraphina and Howard looked at each other and, taking charge, Howard replied, "That is an exceedingly generous offer, but we've lived in London where the crime rate is a lot higher than this. Seraphina is right. We're quite resilient, really. I think we'll be fine. And anyway, it's going to take the glazier a couple of weeks to fix that window. I think we'd be driving you up the wall by then."

Seraphina added in agreement, "Oh gosh, Chris, can you imagine working all day with me and then going home at night as well? It's a very kind offer but I don't even put Howard through that!"

"Well, if you need anything, you must be sure to ring, any time of the day or night," said Ziggy. Flexing his muscles, he continued, "Being quite the power mountain has its advantages sometimes, you know."

"Oh, here he goes again," laughed Chris. "Modesty has always been a quality of yours, hasn't it, Ziggy? Anyway, we really should be going. Has that printer finished yet? I'm excited to read your book."

"Don't forget that it's not finished yet, so the ending still needs to be written, though I've got a few ideas. I'll just nip and check the printer," said Howard, rushing off to the study.

"Come on, Mr Power Mountain. Let's leave these charming people in peace. It's been a lovely evening, Seraphina, and, whatever happens, we should do this more often," said Chris, standing up from the table.

Howard arrived back with almost a ream of A4 paper, saying nervously, "Here you go. Now, just remember, it probably has typos and grammatical errors. This is just my first dirty copy. It's a work in progress, so be gentle with me, won't you?" He passed Chris two copies of his manuscript, each held together with a giant bulldog clip. "I hope this is okay. The clips are all I had. And guys, as you read it, if you find mistakes, please don't be shy; write all over the copy. It really would be very helpful."

Ziggy stood up and, as he pushed the chair back under the table, reassured him, saying, "Don't you worry, I'm all over this and I'll let Chris coordinate with Seraphina regarding our next get-together."

Walking towards the hallway, Howard reached out to shake their hands and thanked them for coming. "No need to be so formal," said Ziggy, as he took his hand and pulled him forwards into a hug. Seraphina quickly interrupted, as she called out, "Hey, where's mine?"

Ziggy turned to Seraphina and wrapping his arms tightly around her, he lifted her completely off the ground. He spun her around in a full circle before putting her down, as he announced, "Everything's going to be great. I just know it. Come on, Chris, let's get out of here before we outstay our welcome."

Opting for the more traditional farewell, Chris shook Howard's hand, and kissed Seraphina on the cheek. "Yes, lovely evening with you both, and take care. Don't forget, you have my number if you get any more grief, day or night."

"Yes, day or night!" Ziggy called as they headed off.

NINETEEN

Saturday evening

Hicks returned to the station and noticed that the inspector's car was still in the car park. Assuming he was still in the building, she resigned herself to the fact she would probably end up sharing her dinner with him. She grabbed two hot chocolates as she passed the vending machine, and with her fish and chips under her arm, she headed to the incident room. As she pushed open the large door with her elbow, the inspector looked up from his desk.

"Well, hello there. I wondered if you'd be back. Is that another hot chocolate you have for me? Oh and dinner too, how thoughtful."

She passed him the drink and he took a large slurp as she unwrapped the fish and chips.

"Ah, nice."

"We can share but next time, Sir, it's your turn to pay for them," she said, pulling some ketchup sachets out of her handbag.

With a hint of amusement in his voice, he said, "Excuse me, I'd like to remind you who treated you to lunch today!" She looked up and was ready to give a sharp answer when she saw him waving a receipt, and looking very pleased with himself.

"When did you get that?"

"Ah, Debbie slipped it to me as we were leaving. She's a keen businesswoman and knows the score. Even so, I can't believe I actually got the receipt this time. I'd better not lose it, like I normally do! Anyway, back to work." He opened his drawer and produced a plastic knife and fork and started on the fish. With a mouth half full he said, "This fish is good. You want to make sure you get some before it goes cold. Now tell me, did you find out anything new at the pub?"

"I must admit, I lost track of time a bit. When I finally got there, the landlady must have already returned to work because there was no answer when I knocked at the side door. I didn't want to make another visit inside, especially on a Saturday night."

"Don't worry about that now. Look, while you've been out enjoying yourself, I've had the results back from forensics on that saucer I acquired. I know, don't scowl at me, but it was important. I had to be sure that Sarah's background checked out, and that Mike was telling me the truth, without attracting any attention to her. Now I can update you about them and their secret.

He flicked open the file with his fork. "You see, Hicks, while you kept Sarah busy in the living room and admired the general decor, Mike told me all about his precious wife. It's not very often we come across someone with a protected identity in our patch, but that's what we have here."

Captivated, she pulled her chair closer to his desk, eager to learn more. "This is so exciting, Sir!"

"I'm not sure if 'exciting' is the right word to use, Hicks. It turns out that Sarah had a bit of a rough start in life. Her father wasn't a very pleasant character. He used to abuse her and her sister, as well as beating her mother. After he went to prison, they moved here for a fresh start. They changed their names and Sarah attended the local school. That's where she met Mike."

Fascinated, but keen to eat before the inspector ate the lot, Hicks asked in between mouthfuls, "So where are her mum and sister then? She never mentioned them today."

"No, she wouldn't have. Thanks to her dad, her sister was in a bad way and needed round-the-clock attention, ending up in a specialist nursing home. A terrible thing, Hicks, terrible. Sadly, she never came out, and she passed away shortly after their mother died. You won't be surprised when I tell you that Sarah struggles with her mental health and Mike's the one who has looked after her. He was understandably wary about confiding in me, as he's kept her secret all these years."

Feeling sorry for Mike, Hicks replied, "It's no wonder that people think he's not a nice person, always so private and appearing moody. But all the time, he's been looking out for her. No wonder he was so friendly when he bumped into me just now."

The inspector wanted to know more. "How was he when you saw him and why didn't you tell me this sooner?"

"I didn't think it was important," she replied, surprised at the urgent tone of his voice. "But I'm telling you now, aren't I? He was in a rush but let me start at the beginning. I tried to get into the pub at the side door but, like I told you, there was no answer. As I stepped back, he came rushing around the corner, bumped into me and knocked me over. It was an accident, and he was very polite and apologetic. He said he was looking for Sarah because she wasn't at home when he got back from town. He asked me to keep an eye out, but he didn't seem too worried and said it wouldn't surprise him if she was already back home when he got there. Why? Is there a problem, Sir?"

"I hope not."

"I did a couple of rounds of the village just to check if I could see her anywhere. After all, she can't have gone far with her ankle in plaster. I didn't see her though and assumed she must have gone back home; then I came here, via the chippy."

"Never mind, Hicks, at least you did a quick check."

Gesturing towards the whiteboard, he continued, "Come on, grab that marker pen. We'll have a look at these boards again. Let's start on the Buchanan case first and brainstorm it. We need to find any clues that might have slipped through the cracks. Start with the note on the brick. What did it say again?" His eyes scanned the room as though he was expecting to find it written down somewhere.

Hicks consulted her notebook, knowing she had written it down earlier. "Ah yes, that's it," she replied and wrote the message in the middle of the board. 'You're not welcome here. Leave now or suffer the consequences.' She circled it with a red marker and then added in black: Seraphina, accountant, job, Howard, no job, pub row, Mike and Sarah Tennant, chemist, new identity, window, brick.

The board had circles within circles and lines branching off in every direction, as well as photos of everyone they had interviewed, and several ominous question marks. Eventually, Hicks sat down next to the inspector's desk, exhausted. "I've racked my brains here, Sir, but I think I'm done. Is there anything else you can think of, or want me to add?"

"Nope, excellent job, Hicks, excellent. I know it's getting late. You've got all the main points up there now. We'll leave that case for the morning but, before we call it a day, or should I say night, why don't you have a quick look through the forensics file just in case you see something I've missed? Fresh eyes and all that. Oh, but only if you can spare the time. Don't forget, we're working for nothing!"

He slid the file over the desk towards her. Gliding faster than expected, he accidentally knocked over his cup of hot chocolate. Hicks jumped up quickly to avoid the mess and stumbled, scattering the file contents across the floor.

Remarkably unphased, the inspector calmly said, "These things happen, Hicks," as he pulled a kitchen roll out of his office drawer. With a cheeky grin, he continued, "Here, use this and, before you say it, yes, this has happened before."

She smiled at him as she took the roll and mopped up the desk, making a mental note to keep drinks away from the inspector when he had files on his desk. She worked her way across the office floor and gradually gathered up the file contents. Glancing briefly at one of the photos she picked up, she wondered how it had got there.

"Sir, look. This must have fallen off the murder board. It's an old photo of poor Andy Pankhurst."

She passed the photo to him and, as he approached the board, he called out urgently, "Hicks, get up here quickly, look at this!"

There was no missing picture on the board. The inspector was holding an old photograph of Sarah

Tennant's father. When they compared it to the murder victim, there was an undeniable resemblance. They stood in silence with their eyes fixed on the photos. As they reached the same conclusion, the inspector cleared his throat and spoke first, his voice low and serious.

"I think maybe you were right yesterday when you asked why anyone would want to kill a guy like him. I think we may have our answer."

Hicks reached over cautiously. "Excuse me, Sir. Can I just take these photos for a minute?" She walked over to the Buchanans' board and neatly lined up the photos of Sarah Tennant's father, Andy Pankhurst and Howard Buchanan.

They stood back in astonishment at another bizarre resemblance. The similarities were undeniable. A shiver ran down Hicks's spine as she realised the gravity of the situation.

"Oh, my god! What were the chances of that? Do you think it might be Sarah, Sir?" asked Hicks.

"I think you're probably right, Hicks, and we need to get to her house as quickly as we can. You drive, but no blue lights or sirens," warned the inspector. "We don't want to scare her away, do we?"

It didn't take them long to get there and as they approached the Tennants' house, the light was just starting to fade. In the distance, they could see the silhouette of a man approaching them at speed on the pavement.

"Look, Sir, I think that's Mike Tennant."

As they got closer, they could see that she was right. Opening the car windows, she stopped the car and called out.

"Hi Mike, it's me, DC Hicks. Have you found Sarah yet?"

"I did, but she snuck out again about half an hour ago." Leaning down to the open car window he looked at the inspector and said, "She's still refusing to take her tablets. When I got back to the house earlier, she had hacked the plaster off her leg and made a right mess. Sarah doesn't like a mess, so it's obvious she's not well and needs help. She's never been this bad before. I'm concerned she might be on the brink of a full-blown psychotic episode. And if she is, who knows what she's capable of?"

The inspector got out of the car and joined Mike. "Now then, don't you worry, Mr Tennant," said the inspector calmly. "We think we know where she might be, so you'd better come with us." He opened the rear passenger door for Mike saying, "Quickly now, we might not have all night."

As the inspector returned to his car seat, Hicks checked, "To the Buchanans' house then, Sir?"

"Yes, turn the car around and, this time, put the lights on but no sirens."

As she drove, the inspector called on the radio for backup and gave Mike a quick synopsis of their theory. Sadly, Mike agreed. "I've been trying to keep her well all these years. Poor Sarah, I'm so sorry."

"Now don't you blame yourself but, when we get there, I'd like you to stay in the car."

******

Meanwhile, Ziggy and Chris had not long left the Buchanans and were wandering home slowly, enjoying the warm evening. "What a fabulous night, Ziggy. Do you think Howard will take you up on his offer?" asked Chris.

"Who knows, but I am certainly looking forward to reading his book. If it's good, I might introduce him to my father. I didn't mention it earlier as I didn't want to get his hopes up."

As Chris looked ahead, he noticed a police car approaching them at considerable speed, with sirens flashing. "Seems like the Old Bill is at it again. I wonder who they're after tonight. It's been a veritable hive of activity here lately, hasn't it? I blame those Buchanan friends of ours." They laughed and Chris jokingly commented, "Don't you think it's funny how the village was such a quiet place until they turned up?"

Ziggy soon stopped laughing when he glanced over his shoulder. "Oh, my god, Chris. I think you might be right. Look, the police have just stopped outside their house!"

"What rubbish are you spouting now?" But, as Chris turned around, he saw that Ziggy was right. They saw two people get out of the car, cross the road, and peer through Howard and Seraphina's front window. As they watched, another two police cars arrived and two more officers ran quickly round to the back of the house.

"Bloody hell! This looks serious, Chris. We must go back, come on." Ziggy marched ahead. When he reached the front door, a police officer who was almost as tall as him grabbed his arm. "Come with me, Sir. You shouldn't go in there just now." With a firm grip on his elbow, he walked Ziggy quickly to the other side of the road, behind the two marked police cars which were positioned as a roadblock.

Catching up, Chris saw what had happened and joined Ziggy behind the cars, asking one of the officers, "What's going on? Our friends are in there. We've only just left them. Are they okay?"

They were desperate to know what was happening. Calmly and quietly, the officer replied, "If you know the residence, then for their sake, it's probably best you let us get on with our job and stay here out of the way or, better still, go home."

"Rude!" announced Ziggy. "We're not going home. We were in there less than half an hour ago. Really, Officer, what can happen in thirty minutes?" He was adamant that he wasn't going anywhere.

Chris spun towards Ziggy with a worried expression etched across his face. "What if it's linked to that smashed window?" he whispered. They exchanged a tense glance but, after a moment's contemplation, they silently agreed to stick around and support their friends.

TWENTY

Saturday late evening

A fter waving Ziggy and Chris off, Howard and Seraphina returned to the kitchen, delighted with their evening. But as they entered the room, they were shocked to see Sarah Tennant sitting on a high stool next to the kitchen island. Their hearts skipped a beat and they stopped dead in their tracks.

Howard was stunned to see that the plaster on Sarah's foot had disappeared, even though her crutches were nearby. Seraphina gasped and shouted defensively, "What the hell are you doing in my house?" She started walking towards Sarah, but Howard quickly grabbed her arm to stop her.

Sarah reached into her pocket and pulled out a long sharp knife which she brandished at Seraphina. Viciously, she spat out, "You stay back. This has nothing to do with you!"

"I think it does. This is my house." Seraphina was firm in her response. "Whatever's going on here concerns me too."

Howard wondered what Sarah was doing in their house. She wasn't her normal self. She looked strange; both scared and enraged. Not like the friendly pretty woman he helped get to the station just a couple of days earlier. But why? He needed to think quickly. He wanted to diffuse the situation and keep his wife safe.

He turned to Seraphina and kept the conversation light-hearted to avoid any escalation. "Let me handle this, Sweetheart. Why don't you pop out for a bit? Maybe you could catch up with Chris and Ziggy? They can't have gone far, and I'll meet you shortly."

Seraphina, however, was adamant that she was standing her ground. "I'm going nowhere without you!"

Nonchalantly, Sarah replied, "You can leave if you like. We don't need you here." Her mood was swinging rapidly, screaming one minute and serene the next.

Howard wanted to draw the attention away from his wife. "There's no need for that knife or violence, is there? Let's have a coffee and talk about whatever has upset you."

Sarah screamed in response, her words dripping with contempt. "No need for violence? Huh! That's rich, coming from you!"

As she shouted at Howard, sweat dripped down her forehead and her hands trembled with a mix of fear and fury. A seething rage was boiling inside her, like a volcano on the brink of eruption. Years of pent-up emotions surged through her body; feelings that the pills had kept buried for so long.

Howard and Seraphina stood frozen, struggling to comprehend what she meant.

"You didn't say that when you were beating up Mum and Annabel!" she spat out, tears streaming down her face.

Howard tried to interject, "Sarah, I believe there's been a misunderstanding."

"Shut up!" she hissed, cutting him off. "You cruel, abusive man. I always knew this day would come. I'm not a child anymore. I'm all grown-up and strong, and it's my turn now." Screaming, she continued to direct her fury at him. "What have you got to say for yourself?" she demanded.

Just then, Howard caught sight of DC Hicks by the kitchen window, who was gesturing towards the back door. Seraphina also noticed.

"What are you two looking at?" Sarah demanded, her voice laced with suspicion. She followed their line of sight and noticed that she'd left the back door open although, fortunately, DC Hicks went unnoticed.

With a menacing wave of the knife, Sarah gestured towards the door. "You, woman, lock that door."

Howard attempted to reason with her. "But Sarah, didn't you suggest we let Seraphina go? You don't need her, do you?"

A wicked grin spread across Sarah's face as she brandished the knife in his direction. "I've got a much better idea." Her eyes flashed with a twisted glee. "Why don't I do to her what you did to Mum? Then you can suffer the same mental torture I've endured all these years." Her screams echoed through the room as she demanded that Howard should move away from Seraphina and stand in the corner. His heart raced with fear as he reluctantly complied, wondering what horrors she had in store for his wife.

With a sharp turn towards Seraphina, Sarah's eyes blazed with fury. Her voice was low and menacing as she demanded, "Why haven't you locked that door yet? Do it now!"

The urgency in her tone conveyed a sense of impending danger, which frightened Seraphina. As she gingerly made her way towards the door, she kept her distance from Sarah. Just as she was about to pass her, she stumbled on the crutches and lost her footing. The fall filled her with a sense of terror and she frantically tried to get back on her feet, unsure of what might happen next.

The sudden fall frayed Sarah's nerves further. With fierce strength and a complete disregard for her ankle, she leapt off the stool and slammed her knee into Seraphina's back, returning her to the floor with considerable force, and leaving her gasping for air. She seized her hair, yanked her head back and held the knife to her throat. Seraphina's heart pounded with fear as she realised that she was at Sarah's mercy; terrified of what she might do next.

Fearing for his wife's life, Howard couldn't stop himself from stepping forward.

"Don't come any closer!" shrieked Sarah. He froze on the spot as she yelled at him, "How dare you call yourself a dad!"

Howard's heart was pounding as he watched her carelessly swing the blade close to Seraphina's neck. "I wonder," Sarah said, as she continued to wave the knife, her voice low and menacing, "how pretty her face would be if I just did a little etching on it."

Howard held his breath. He knew that one wrong move would put his wife in mortal danger.

Sarah noticed Seraphina's exposed wrists and, moving the knife away from her neck, said, "Or I could make one deep clean cut here. It would be quick and she wouldn't feel a thing. If it doesn't hurt, it didn't really happen, did it, Daddy?" Her voice cracked as she tried to hold back the tears.

Realising that she was suffering from some kind of episode, Howard tried again to talk to her calmly. "I can see you've been through a lot but I think you're mistaken. Look at me." He patted his chest with both hands. "I'm Howard Buchanan. We met at the corner shop, remember? And that's my wife, Seraphina, you're sitting on."

Out of the corner of his eye, he could see DC Hicks once again positioned in the back doorway. Buying time to figure out what to do, he continued, "Sarah, you're not yourself. Please do the right thing and put the knife down. Look, I'm even going to step away to show you how much I trust you."

Sarah was confused and, as she stopped to think, her attention momentarily shifted from the knife as she tried to make sense of things. Seraphina glared at him with wide eyes as she felt it scratch her wrist. He carefully stepped to the left and, by doing so, changed Sarah's peripheral view. He felt sure that DC Hicks could now enter unseen.

"There, is that okay, Sarah? Now let's talk, please."

"Talk to you? What is there to say?" With tears rolling down her cheeks, she looked at the knife which had slipped and broken the skin. A single drop of blood ran down Seraphina's hand.

"Come on, Sarah, you're amongst friends. Why not put down the knife? You're safe here."

As she looked at Howard, Sarah's confusion turned into a full-blown rage. She clenched her fists as she pulled Seraphina's hair tighter, shouting back, "Safe? Huh! Safe? How dare you say that! We were NEVER safe with you." Her voice was shaking with anger, as were her hands.

Hicks sensed the tension emanating from behind the door. She knew it would only take one false move to trigger

Sarah, but she needed to act soon. Checking over her shoulder for backup, she signalled for them to stand by. She crept into the kitchen and, approaching Sarah from behind, called at the top of her voice, "Now!"

The next thirty seconds felt like an eternity to Howard. The air was thick with tension as Sarah's face twisted with torment and shock at the sound of Hicks's voice. Suddenly, she raised the knife high above her head, ready to strike Seraphina with all her might.

Howard's heart raced as he watched in horror. Before he could process what was happening, Hicks had lunged forward and grabbed Sarah's arm from behind. Startled, she released Seraphina and twisted herself around to face Hicks, her grip on the knife tightening.

The scramble that followed resulted in a full-body roll across the kitchen floor. It ended when Sarah and Hicks banged up against the wall and the knife slid across the flagstones. As Howard rushed to his wife's side, he turned to see Sarah and Hicks lying motionless, momentarily stunned. The sound of shouting and scrambling soon filled the air as uniformed officers moved in to help subdue Sarah.

"About time," said Hicks to the officers, as she peeled herself off Sarah. "Cuff her please," she instructed and, as she stood up, revealed a pool of blood slowly spreading across the floor.

"Let me in! Where is she?" demanded Mike Tennant, who was now standing at the back door, having followed the inspector.

"All in good time, Sir. Please return to the car," replied the inspector. Undeterred, Mike pushed his way past him and several police officers and rushed to his wife's side, where he dropped to his knees.

"Oh, my god, Sarah. Speak to me, please." Taking hold of her tightly, he felt his jeans soak up the seeping blood as she gazed at him.

"Can we get a medic here quickly, please?" called the inspector, as he walked up to the knife lying on the kitchen floor. He pulled out a clean white handkerchief from his pocket and picked it up. "Anyone have a specimen bag?" he asked, dangling the knife in the air.

Seraphina turned to Howard as an officer ushered them into an ambulance. "I never knew our kitchen could hold so many people." Soon, they were wrapped in blankets to keep warm as the inspector approached them. "Here, I made us all a nice hot sweet drink." Smiling, he handed them each a cup. "Your kitchen is lovely when it's not so full. I'm sure we'll all be out of your hair soon and the officers will have this cleared up in no time."

As they sipped their tea, they watched Sarah being wheeled out on a trolley into another waiting ambulance. Mike held her hand and looked back at the inspector but remained silent. The doors closed, and the ambulance left at speed.

"Do you think Sarah will be okay, Inspector?" Seraphina asked.

"Well, it's not a nice wound but I don't think it will do any long-term damage. Although, I think Sarah has more than just a knife wound that needs mending. It's such a shame." He paused as he sipped his drink. "Oh, before I forget, there are a couple of men over there claiming to be your friends, pestering the officers and asking after you.

Chris and Zippy, I think their names were. Should I send them away?"

They both laughed and Seraphina corrected him. "Ziggy, that will be Ziggy."

"Well, there you go. You're clearly feeling better already."

Turning to the officers, the inspector called out, "I think you'd better let them through now."

He stood up and, with a cheeky grin, held out his empty teacup for Howard. "I believe this is yours. I'll call around in the morning to wrap things up with you. In the meantime, try to stay out of trouble and get some rest. Oh and, I just like to reassure you, it's not every day that something like this happens. This is usually such a lovely tranquil place to live. Village life isn't always murder, you know."

Chris arrived just in time to overhear the last comment. "Murder! Are you two okay? We've been ever so worried about you."

Ziggy took one look at them. "I can see you've had quite an ordeal. We can't leave you alone for five minutes, can we? Or was it ten?" he joked. "Anyway, as long as you're both all right, that's all that matters. We can catch up with you in a few days, can't we Chris?" It was more of an instruction than a suggestion.

"Yes, Seraphina, why not take a couple of days off?" said Chris.

Anticipating a potential refusal, Howard swiftly cut in, "Thanks, Chris. That's a fantastic idea, don't you think, Seraphina?"

"Yes. Thank you, Chris, that's very thoughtful of you, and thanks for coming back to check on us. I'll see you in the office in a couple of days then."

"Sorted. We'll leave you in peace and see you soon." Ziggy said, leaning forward and giving Seraphina a quick peck on the cheek.

"Well, it looks like my work here is done Mr Buchanan, so I'll say goodnight too," interrupted the inspector "Come on Hicks, you can drive me home."

As they walked to their car, Howard could hear the Inspector handing out tasks for Hicks to do until they were out of earshot. "Oh, and don't forget to cancel that request for uniform at the station for Monday. I don't think we'll be needing them now. Oh, and on the google, can you…"

Howard and Seraphina watched the last police car drive away, and their road returned to its usual tranquil state.

"What a night, Seraphina, what a night. Come on, let's head inside and get a plaster on that cut."

TWENTY-ONE

A few days later

The inspector kept his promise and called on Sunday morning to finalise Howard and Seraphina's statements. With the weight of the incident lifted from their shoulders, they spent the next few days talking about their future together.

The 'Sarah incident' had brought their relationship into the limelight, and they both needed to bottom out what they wanted for their future. Eventually, they arrived at a mutual decision.

"Okay, that's settled. I'll call Chris and let him know I'll be back at work tomorrow, and we can invite them over for dinner," Seraphina said confidently.

She wasted no time and immediately made the call. "Hi, Chris. Yes, everything is back to normal here. I'm feeling fine, thank you. I'm perfectly fit to return to work, otherwise, I wouldn't be calling you. Howard agrees too. Great, I'm glad that's all sorted."

Chris was eager to see them but he didn't want to impose, so he cautiously asked, "If it's all right with you, and you're both feeling up to it, would you like to come to our place for dinner this evening?"

"Oh, I was just about to suggest the same thing! Hold on a minute, let me check with Howard," Seraphina laughed.

She called out to Howard and relayed the offer, before grabbing a pen and notepad. "We would love to accept your kind offer. What time should we come over? Oh, and could you please give me your address?"

"Let's say 6:30 pm, shall we? It's a school night, after all. And don't worry about my address. I'll send a car to your house. Bye."

The line disconnected before she could utter another word. Excited, she hurried through the house to find Howard. "Guess what? They're sending a car to collect us! A chauffeur, no less. I wonder why? Howard, are you listening?"

"Yes, I heard you. How nice. But spending all day wondering why won't make any difference, will it? Just enjoy your last day off, Sweetheart."

She knew he was right and kept herself busy for the rest of the day with housework. Bleaching the stone kitchen floor, for the third time in as many days, she finally removed the last traces of blood. Meanwhile, Howard spent most of his day typing away in the study, displaying a level of motivation that Seraphina hadn't seen in years.

At 6:15 pm, the doorbell rang, and she hurried to answer it, filled with the same excitement as a child on Christmas morning. She was eager to see the car and its driver. As she opened the front door, a chauffeur dressed in a traditional uniform tipped his cap at her and announced, "Car for Mr and Mrs Buchanan," before stepping away from the entrance to wait next to the silver Rolls Royce.

Seraphina didn't need to be asked twice. She got into the car before Howard had even locked the front door.

In no time, they were travelling down a long, tree-lined driveway. Eventually, the car parked in front of a large country house. As they got out of the car, Chris and Ziggy came out to greet them, all hugs and kisses.

Ziggy gushed, "So nice to see you both again, my darlings. Do come in, and I'll get us some drinks."

As he ushered them into the drawing room, a tall impeccably-dressed man of mature years entered the room carrying a tray of drinks. Howard and Seraphina were stunned by the grandeur of the house and that their friends had both a chauffeur and a butler.

Howard whispered to Seraphina, "Close your mouth, my dear."

Ziggy burst out laughing. "What an entrance you always make, Dad. You must stop winding people up like that." He turned to Howard and Seraphina and announced, "So, just to put your mind at rest, this isn't the resident butler. Let me introduce you to Mr Palmer Senior, or 'Dad' to me. You don't mind if he joins us, do you?"

Suddenly Seraphina remembered the description that Howard had read out the other day. 'Ziggy Palmer, son of the self-made millionaire, someone or other.' She kicked herself for not having the patience to listen to the rest when he offered to read it out. Feeling a little star-struck, but trying to appear cool, she introduced herself to Ziggy's father as she accepted a glass of something bubbly off the tray.

"Of course, we don't mind. How nice to meet you, Mr Palmer, and thank you for the drink. I'm Seraphina, and this is my long-suffering husband, Howard, although I expect Ziggy has already told you that, hasn't he? You know, you fooled me there for a minute, especially after the ride in the car."

She could see where Ziggy got his good looks from. The years had been kind to Mr Palmer Senior. He was tall and handsome, with a wicked sense of humour. She wondered if Ziggy had also inherited his charm.

Mr Palmer placed the tray down on a nearby table and directed his attention towards her, raising his eyebrows as a cheeky grin spread across his face. "Yes, sorry about that. Although the car is mine. Come on now, no need to stand on show. Please, have a seat, and rest your beautiful self, my dear."

There's the charm, she thought to herself, as she took a seat on the large velvet sofa, followed by Mr Palmer Senior. Sitting unexpectedly close to her, he took hold of one of her hands and cradled it.

"Now then, young lady, Ziggy and Chris mentioned how you and Howard have recently had the most extraordinary ordeal. It takes incredible strength to overcome such events and, from what I hear, you have that by the bucket-load. So, it seems to me that you're not only a fighter but a true beauty as well. What a lucky man your husband is."

Feeling flattered and slightly embarrassed by his charm, she took a large sip of her drink as she looked across the room at Howard.

Ziggy laughed as he handed his dad a drink. "Come on, you old fool. Leave her alone. But yes, Dad, we've both been eager to hear all the details. There's nothing like getting the information straight from the horse's mouth, is there? I've been relying on social media, but Chris went to the corner shop and got the full story from June. How accurate that is, though, I'm not entirely sure."

Howard joined the conversation. "I haven't been down there yet. I decided it was probably best to stay away for a few days. I bet June and Barbara have been having a field day; you know what they're like. It's probably like you said the other day, Ziggy. All the time they're talking about us, they're leaving someone else alone."

"That's the right attitude," Chris said, rubbing his stomach. "Follow me, guys. Let's go through to the dining room. I'm starving."

During dinner, Howard and Seraphina shared the harrowing details of their ordeal. Howard concluded, "I'm not sure what's going to happen to Sarah now, after all, she did kill that poor chap at the train station, and given half a chance she would have killed me too. Being a lookalike is not such a good thing around here is all I can say. But joking apart, the future does look bleak for her. I think she's currently in a secure hospital."

"I feel sorry for her husband," Seraphina added.

"It seems to me, that the only thing he ever did wrong was to love her," said Mr Palmer Senior.

"You old romantic Dad," added Ziggy.

As everyone finished their meals, Seraphina placed her knife and fork neatly on the spotlessly clean plate, saying, "I'm stuffed. It's definitely not the Indian takeaway we were expecting. That's got to be one of the best meals I've had this side of Italy. I'm booking myself into this restaurant again."

"It was our pleasure," Ziggy said, looking at Chris. "It's a little hobby of ours. We love cooking together, but your appreciation and gratitude makes us very happy."

Chris looked up, giggling. "You're always so dramatic, Ziggy. For a moment, I thought you were going to launch into a speech." Tutting at Chris, Ziggy continued, "Anyway, let's see if we can make you happy as well. Not a speech this time, but a proposition."

Seraphina looked confused. "I'm stumped. Another proposition, or are we still talking about your offer the other day?"

"Ok, well, let's call it an amended proposition." Ziggy took a deep breath. "So, this is what I wanted to say. When we started reading your book …"

Howard sat bolt upright and suddenly felt nervous. He grabbed Seraphina's hand and squeezed it tightly, waiting in anticipation of what they would say.

"None of us could put it down. It's a brilliant story, a great plot and we can't wait to read the final few chapters." Howard was confused. "Did you say 'none of us', don't you mean 'neither of us'?"

"Oh, get you Howard, getting all literal and precise, you author you," Seraphina teased.

"Well, Seraphina, to be honest, Howard is right. We're not the only ones to have read his book. I must confess that we haven't been entirely truthful with you both," explained Ziggy, as he paused to gauge their reactions before continuing.

"You see, when Chris and I read your book, even without an ending, we could see it was brilliant and worthy of publishing. So, we ran it by Polly, one of the talent scouts at Dad's company."

Seraphina's eyebrows couldn't get any higher with surprise. Howard was confused and excited at the same time and kept his eyes firmly fixed on Ziggy, too nervous to think about what he was going to say next.

"You weren't to have known, but Dad owns Emanuels, the publishing company. Impressed, Polly told Dad about it. Since we were planning to visit him anyway, we thought it would be an excellent opportunity to invite you over and introduce you. Oh yes, another thing I didn't say, this is Dad's house; ours isn't quite so grand. Anyway, he always likes to meet promising authors and, well, here we all are. Over to you now, Dad, the ball's in your court."

All eyes turned to Mr Palmer Senior. "Thank you for the introduction, my dear son. You're absolutely right, this manuscript has incredible potential. Allow me to open our discussion by offering you a three-book deal. As I understand it, you'll have ample time on your hands as you intend to manage my son's new gallery." He looked at Ziggy and laughed so loudly it echoed through the room, as he playfully teased his son. "Those places are always like crematoriums, anyway."

Ziggy rolled his eyes and replied, "Dad, Howard has yet to accept my proposal."

All eyes turned to Howard. Trying to take it all in, he picked up his glass and took a large gulp. The room was silent as he looked around the table. He took hold of Seraphina's hand and gave it a little squeeze of excitement. Eventually he spoke. "Well, Ziggy, we have given your offer some serious consideration, and it was very tempting."

He paused, realising everyone was hanging on his every word. He wanted to build suspense by making them wait longer, but he couldn't contain himself. He smiled and nodded his head at Seraphina before he turned to them all.

"I'm overwhelmed. I was going to accept your offer anyway, Ziggy. Now with this offer from your dad, I don't know what to say, apart from yes, a great big yes, and thank you. Thank you all so very much."

"That's great. No more of this Prosecco rubbish. I'm off to get the champagne," announced Ziggy.

"Don't forget, you've got to write the end of that book yet," said Chris as he handed round the champagne.

"Oh yes, I'll do that tomorrow. I think, just for now, I'm going to enjoy the moment." Howard held up his glass to everyone and announced, "A toast, everyone. To great friends." They chinked their glasses and repeated, "To great friends."

Seraphina almost burst with pride as she looked at him. She was so happy. She had her Howard back; the successful man she had married all those years ago. She couldn't stop herself. She jumped up and kissed him, before announcing, "You know what, Howard? Maybe this bloody village life isn't so bad after all."

THE END

ACKNOWLEDGEMENTS

I must firstly thank my wonderful husband for his unwavering faith in me. Whilst I may have written this book, without him it would never have made it to print. The patience he has with me is unparalleled. For every hour I have spent on this book he has been left to his own devices. As so I guess it must follow that I should thank his friends and work colleagues for keeping him entertained in my absence.

I would also like to thank my daughter, Katrina, who gave me the confidence to continue, reassuring me that what I had written was *"actually really good"*.

So many other people have helped me along the way. My friends, Sue and Michelle were brave enough to read my first, very rough manuscript, and encouraged me to continue, and more importantly, are still my friends. Many others have read chapters for me along the way, for which I am very thankful.

I will be forever grateful to my editor, Christine Beech, as without her I would never have felt brave enough to publish. Also, my typesetter, Matt Bird, for not only pulling it all together and making it look like a real book, but also his patience in helping me to get it published.

I would also like to thank Michael Heppell and his "*Write That Book*" course. Apparently, his books have been published in 27 different languages worldwide, so not a bad mentor to have. Without a shadow of a doubt, this book would never be in print today had it not been for him. Plus all the lovely people I met through the course, who have all helped me in different ways and also deserve a mention: Nicky, Erika, Charmaine, Debra, Elaine, Jane, Judith, Lis, Mark and Sam. Together we made a formidable team and if not already, are fast on their way to becoming authors too.

About the Author

Originally from Kent, growing up mainly in the West Midlands, Penelope has made her home in a quiet country village in the East Midlands. She loves to escape her day job in financial services by being creative.

When she's not messing around on her allotment with her flowers, you'll find her in the kitchen baking or crafting. Plus she has never given up hope of one day mastering the piano.

Printed in Great Britain
by Amazon